Echoes of the Damned

Ian Gielen

ISBN: 978-1-7640126-2-1
Cover designed by Matthew Wildasin
Edited by Tory Favro
Formatted by Jyl Glenn
Published by Ian Gielen

To my son, to whom I first showed the cover of this collection, the first cover I'd ever gotten made and shared the excitement with me. I love you with every ounce of my being.

"The evil that men do lives after them; the good is oft interred with their bones." — William Shakespeare, Julius Caesar

ACKNOWLEDGMENTS

This collection is a special one for me as it represents how I started off on my writing journey. Back about three years ago now, I started my writing career off with seeing a submission call on the Books of Horror Facebook page for an anthology, the "Books of Horror Community Anthology Volume 4". Having always wanted to try my hand at writing since my teenage years, I decided to try my hand at it, not expecting to get in, just wanting to experience writing a full story from start to finish.

It was a huge surprise to learn a few months later that I was accepted. From that point forward, I was hooked. There were a few stops and starts along the way, but I continued to write short stories, submitting them where I could and learning about the business along the way. Some of these stories were those that I wrote during that time but have been reworked and revised a little to include my learnings since those days.

I want to thank Tory Favro, a fellow Australian author who has some amazing books out there that everyone should read, for his efforts in editing and giving me feedback on these stories so that I could have the opportunity to improve them. Not only is he a fantastic writer, but he is a friend that I appreciate dearly.

Thanks also to Matthew Wildasin who has waited patiently for me to get this done so I could finally make use of the brilliant cover he made for me well over a year ago.

And thanks once again to Jyl Glenn for her formatting work on this collection. She is someone I am grateful to call a friend and is also an amazing author. Everyone should check out her work and the anthology she put together with Savannah Fischer.

Here is where I list the works and where they first appeared. There are some fantastic stories in these anthologies, so definitely check them out if you get a chance.

"Ghostly Desires" was originally published in *Children of the Dead: Lost Lullabies* by Wicked Shadow Press in September 2024

"Mind Games" was originally published in *Invasion of the Saucer-Men from Mars!* by Specul8 Publishing in July 2024

"Masked Rage" was originally published in *Masks of Sanity: The Monster Within* by Wicked Shadow Press in May 2024

"The Moon's Kiss" was originally published in *Apocalyptales: Judgement Day* by Wicked Shadow Press in January 2024

"Deadly Bytes" was originally published in *Warning: Wicked Web* by Crimson Cult Media in January 2025

"One Night in Halloween Land" was originally published in *Halloweenthology: Trick-Or-Treat* by Wicked Shadow Press in October 2023

Contents

Ghostly Desires

Anna's eyes fluttered open to the gentle touch of warm sunlight seeping through the cracks of her bedroom window, casting a soothing radiance that filled the space. Sitting up, she couldn't help but let out a big yawn, feeling the sleepiness fade away as she stretched her body. It took a few minutes for her to remember that it was the weekend, but when she did, a rush of excitement filled her, giving her the energy to jump out of bed and start her morning routine.

Since moving into her new house a few months ago, Anna had struggled to make friends, but just yesterday she had made her first one in her school, and found to her delight, that she only lived a street away, across the other side of the cemetery. *It was time for a playdate*, she had decided. Samantha didn't know about it yet, but Anna was sure she'd be just as excited about it as she was.

Anna, at nine years old, had more freedom than most other girls her age, giving her the opportunity to explore the area as soon as they moved in. She and her mother were always moving, and though she found it tiresome to continuously change schools and try to make new friends, she also enjoyed exploring each new place they moved to. She liked to find places that no-one else knew about, wild places where she could behave as she liked and not worry about adults who were constantly on her back about her bad attitude and behaviour. Those were the places she felt the most relaxed but it was lonely sometimes. So naturally, whenever she made new friends, she invited them to come join her. Now it was time to reveal to Samantha the most special place she had discovered in this town so far.

Rushing through her morning routine, she quickly put on her favorite dress, decorated with cheerful flowers that matched the vibrancy of the sunny day, and hurried downstairs. Before she disappeared out the front door, she grabbed a slice of cold toast smeared with margarine and honey from the kitchen table on her way past and waved goodbye to her stepmom. The door swung open in her wake, and the crisp, cool air of fall rushed into the lounge room.

Janet, Anna's stepmother, stood motionless in the kitchen, her eyes staring after Anna, her gaze vacant as she watched the swirling wind depositing leaves onto the floor of the lounge room.

There was a palpable sense of exhaustion and sorrow to her, as if she had been carrying the weight of the world on her shoulders. She knew now that soon they would have to move again, now that Anna had found a new friend.

Leaning against the kitchen doorframe with a sigh, her thoughts turned as they always did to how much she missed John, her husband. He had always had a way with Anna, a way to soothe her untamed spirit. Now that he was gone, there was no stopping her.

Anna skipped joyfully along the winding path that led towards the cemetery. She had often visited there, enjoying the quiet until someone inevitably came along and spoiled it to lay some flowers at the foot of a grave. Grownups had always spoiled her fun, especially her dad. Well, not real dad. Stepdad. He was gone now though. Sometimes that thought hurt, and she missed him. Most other times, she was glad. She knew she shouldn't think like that, but she couldn't help it. She had always been different from other children and thought about things differently too.

According to some special doctors she had to go visit with her stepmom and stepdad, it was because of how she was raised by her mom. Anna spent her early childhood in a cult, where her mother held a special position, until some angry-looking people dressed in strange clothes took her mom away to prison. Her mom had also been a heavy user of drugs during her pregnancy.

Anna knew about drugs. She had taken a fascination to them when she found out they could make you feel and act a certain way. She liked that. It was fun seeing her mom acting all goofy and silly when she took her special medicine.

Sudden movement out of the corner of her eye made her turn towards a large, old-looking concrete building in the distance. She stopped for a moment to take a longer look, her eyes widening in surprise when she recognized what it was. It was Susan, her friend from the town she had just moved from. She was standing there staring at her as if she were a stranger, her dress fluttering in the breeze. Eager to get to Samantha's house, Anna flashed a quick wave to her before pressing on.

When she realized she was near the end of the cemetery, her excitement grew, knowing that Samantha's street was nearby. Just as she was about to head toward the exit, her eyes caught sight of Millie, another one of her friends. She was one of the first friends Anna had made since her stepdad had died.

She was standing next to a plain-looking gravestone. Like Susan, she too stared at Anna silently, not even a hint of a smile on her face. "How rude," Anna muttered to herself, giving Millie a wave anyway out of courtesy before moving towards the exit.

Skipping out the gate at the end of the cemetery, she looked both ways for cars before crossing the street, scanning the house numbers. Samantha had been initially reluctant to tell Anna her house number, but eventually caved in and said she lived at number forty-seven. The street she found herself on was in a sorry state, with houses that looked ancient and neglected. Through the window of a house she passed, she noticed an old lady glaring at her, her wrinkled face frowning with disapproval. What was with these old people? She shrugged. They were so creepy!

She was used to frowns. She had seen so many of them directed at her that they made her angry. They were usually followed by someone yelling at her. Pausing for a moment, she stuck her tongue out and made a silly face, with her thumbs in her ears and her fingers wiggling. With a shake of her head, the old lady closed the curtain, her face twisted in a look of disgust. Anna grinned. It was always fun to get a rise out of people; it made her feel good. Made her feel... alive.

Whistling to herself, she resumed skipping and counted the house numbers until she arrived at the right one. Number forty-seven. Among the row of houses, this one appeared no different, except for the neglected yard next to it, where tall grass swayed, and an unruly tree awaited pruning. *Samantha's family must be poor,* she thought to herself. If they allow the house to look like this, her parents couldn't be good people either.

With a disappointed shake of her head, Anna rushed up to the front door and pressed the doorbell. To her annoyance, there was no sound. It must've been broken. She sighed and rapped on the thin window loudly and waited impatiently, resuming her whistling.

A few moments later, the door creaked open, and Samantha greeted her with a hesitant smile, her lips twitching and reflecting uncertainty.

"Anna? What are you doing here?"

"What do you mean, silly? I told you I'd come by today. I want to show you something super special. You know, the place I told you about yesterday?" With a laugh, Anna couldn't help but shake her head at the silliness of Samantha.

"But I said I couldn't come today. My dad is working a long way away, and my mom is visiting her friend a few houses away."

Anna pouted, her expression darkening.

"You're ruining everything. The place I want to show you is special. I don't just invite anyone, you know."

"Can't we go another day?"

"No, this is the only chance I'm giving you. If you're really my friend, you'll come."

Samantha sighed, her eyes flickering with unease.

"Is it far away?"

In an instant, Anna's face transformed, a wide smile spreading across her features as her voice became filled with an infectious excitement.

"No, it's not. It's very close. I bet we could go and come back before your mom even knows you went anywhere."

With a mix of hesitation and nervousness, Samantha fidgeted in the doorway, shifting from one foot to the other. Finally, she glanced up at Anna, offering a shy smile as her cheeks flushed a soft pink, adding a touch of innocence to her expression.

"Well... OK. If it's really going to be quick, then I suppose it won't hurt."

"No, it won't hurt, I promise."

Anna's face conveyed sincerity, her body language relaxed and open, inviting trust.

"Cross my heart and hope to die."

Anna exaggerated her movements as Samantha laughed shyly, her laughter sounding soft and forced.

Stepping outside, Samantha closed the door halfway before pausing uncertainly, her eyes darting between Anna and the interior of the house.

"Wait... I just need to get my jacket. I'll be right back."

Without waiting for a reply, she dashed back inside, the door slamming shut behind her.

Anna's anger grew at the delay. If Samantha was going to be her friend, she needed to know that she shouldn't anger Anna. It was a lesson Anna would have to teach her. A very important lesson.

She sighed; she hated teaching others how to behave. Why couldn't they just do what she wanted them to do? Think the same way she thought?

Growing increasingly impatient, she raised herself onto her tiptoes and strained to peer through the window of the door. Samantha was standing there at the kitchen table, her jacket already on and scribbling something on a piece of paper. Was she writing a note to her parents? The thought intensified her already simmering anger, turning it into a blazing fire. This was taking too long. Samantha was taking too long.

After what felt like an eternity to Anna, the door creaked open, and Samantha emerged.

"Sorry I took so long. I forgot where my jacket was," she said with a high-pitched nervous laugh.

Stiffening at the lie, Anna's face momentarily became devoid of expression before breaking into a smile in response.

"That's okay. Let's go. I can't wait until you see this place."

Holding Samantha's hand firmly, Anna led her reluctant friend behind her as they walked along the street. They continued until they reached the end and entered a small park, where they saw a few parents chatting while their children played on the swings.

"Is this it?" Samantha asked, her eyebrows knitting together in a frown.

"Of course not, silly. It's behind here. We have to go over a fence to get there."

Halting in her tracks, Samantha released Anna's hand, her face turning pale, her eyes darted back and forth, torn between the fence and Anna.

"I don't think we should do that. We could get in trouble."

Annoyed, Anna let out a huff of exasperation.

"You worry too much. We won't get in trouble. I've been there lots of times. It's fine, I promise."

Samantha's gaze fell to the ground, her frown deepening as she squirmed uneasily, pressing her shoe into the dirt and twisting it, as if searching for answers.

"Please? It would mean the world to me if you came."

Samantha looked up at Anna, feeling reassured by

the warmth of her gentle, almost vulnerable smile, and finally gave in with a nod.

"Yay!" Anna exclaimed joyfully.

"Let's go. The fence is just past these trees here."

The pair walked through the cluster of trees at the end of the park to reveal a rickety-looking wire fence. The fence-line had seen better days, with half of the wire detached from the decayed posts, creating an unsteady tilt towards the ground.

"See? It's easy. Just follow me."

Hand in hand, Anna and Samantha ventured toward a part of the wire fence that seemed to bow down, beckoning them to explore. Anna stepped over the wire, making sure to avoid the protruding parts, and pulled Samantha along with her.

Unlike Anna, Samantha's steps were less steady, and she found herself stepping on an upturned piece of wire, which immediately ensnared her foot. Anna stumbled, thrown off balance by Samantha's sudden stop, her dress snagging on the wiring and ripping a hole in the delicate fabric.

"No! Oh no, look what you've done!" she screamed, her face turning red, her eyes wide and filled with panic, as she pulled at the ends of her dress to inspect the damage.

"You've ruined my dress. My favorite dress."

Anna dropped to her knees, stricken, tears flowing down her face as she gazed at the tear in her dress.

"I... I'm sorry," Samantha said. "I didn't mean to, I swear. I just got stuck in the wire."

Anna stopped crying and looked up at her with a cold, piercing stare, her lips pressed tightly together, her eyes filled with anger, and her tear-streaked cheeks flushed.

"You better buy me a new one. You owe me now."

Samantha nodded, her eyes downcast, her fingers fumbling as she struggled to free herself from the tangled wire.

Anna stood up abruptly, not saying a word, her face still betraying her anger, and marched off into the woods, leaving Samantha to free herself.

Her voice cracked. "Anna, wait!". She was struck by the harsh reality of the situation. She was alone in a place she wasn't supposed to be in, having left her house with no one knowing her whereabouts or destination, and her new friend, whom she didn't know very well, had abandoned her.

Samantha tugged her foot frantically, feeling the wire give a little with each pull until it tore free, leaving deep scratches on her new leather shoes her mother had bought her just a few weeks ago.

The sight moved her to tears, her shoulders heaving with each sob. More than anything now, she just wanted to go home. She decided she would find Anna and tell her before she did.

With a sniffle, she wiped away the tears pooling at the corner of her eyes, the raw emotion evident on her trembling lips, and began to follow the trail Anna had left behind. After a few more sniffles, she walked on in silence. The only sounds left accompanying her were the startled, agitated twittering of birds and the rapid fluttering of their wings.

A few minutes later, she emerged into a clearing. Before her, the edge of a cliff offered a breathtaking view beyond, of a valley dotted with rolling hills, patches of forest, and scattered sheep and cows. A river snaked through the valley, making its way toward the cliff she stood on and followed its base, its fast-moving water driven by a powerful current.

"Anna?" Samantha called out, scanning the clearing and the cliff edge for any sign of her.

As she neared the cliff edge, a wave of unease washed over her. She squinted her eyes, searching for any sign of Anna's presence, but she was nowhere to be seen.

Right as she was considering turning back, a sudden and powerful shove sent her stumbling toward the edge, her feet tripping over the rocks that lined the way. Fear coursed through her as she let out a gasp and a piercing cry, unable to stop herself from tumbling over the edge. In a desperate attempt to save herself, she twisted and extended her hands, grabbing onto the edge and found herself suspended dangerously above the raging river below.

"Anna, help! Help me!" she screamed in panic, her whole-body trembling with shock as she attempted to hoist herself up, but her efforts were futile. She just wasn't strong enough.

Anna's face, bright with a smile, appeared above her, her eyes filled with a hint of excitement.

"You silly. You almost fell into the river. It's so beautiful here, isn't it? I told you it was worth it."

"Please help me," Samantha cried, her eyes meeting Anna's in a heart-wrenching last-ditch plea, as she felt her grip weaken.

Anna looked down at her, her smile fading as she tilted her head to the side curiously, her eyes narrowing in a cold, calculating look.

This was the most exciting part of making friends. When she had the most fun. It was also the hardest. She could already picture her stepdad in her mind, his stern voice reminding her that she had a responsibility to help her friend. To be a real friend to others was to care for them and their well-being. All the lectures and teachings her stepdad had drilled into her played over in her mind, but they didn't matter anymore. He was gone. She could still see his face twisted in surprise, the way his hand had reached for her before falling limp. She had taught him a lesson of her own, that she didn't need his guidance anymore.

Though he wasn't physically there anymore, she still saw him sometimes. Standing there beside her stepmom, glaring at Anna in anger and raising his finger at her as if in disappointment. Her mind wandered to her other friends, and a wave of happiness washed over her. All the friends she'd met since that day she still saw. They followed her everywhere she moved. They couldn't do much more than stand there and mouth things toward her, looking frightened, scared or angry on account of not having bodies anymore, but they filled her with comfort, knowing how many friends she had. She would soon have another friend like that.

The sight of Samantha's terrified face below her filled her with a tingling sensation of anticipation.

"Please help me," Samantha pleaded once more, her face drained of color, perspiration trickling down her forehead as she desperately clung on.

"I will," Anna whispered softly, her fingers gently prying apart Samantha's grip.

"I will help you become my friend forever."

The Scientist's Curse

10 Years Ago
Ouachita National Forest, Hot Springs, AR

"Found 'im," Buster called out, spotting his quarry dart between the trees ahead. He grinned, his eyes wild and full of excitement. Judging by the amount of blood littering the trail left behind in their prey's wake, it wouldn't be long before the hunt would be over.

"Wish he would slow down a little. I ain't as fit as I once were," Hank said, stumbling through the bushes behind Buster. He bent over in exhaustion, using the ground to support the butt of his rifle while resting his other hand on his thighs. Hank gasped for breath while Buster leaned against his shotgun, chuckling and shaking his head.

"You need to lay off the Jack and Coke a bit I reckon," Buster said, bumping Hank's shoulder with his own hard enough to send Hank sprawling face first into the bushes.

His hearty laughter resounded in the woods as he doubled over, slapping his thigh in amusement.

"You ain't gonna catch anything down there."

He continued to bellow with laughter, his booming guffaws echoing through the forest.

"You's an asshole, ya know that?" Hank grumbled as he sat up, wiping leaves off his shoulder.

His response only heightened Buster's amusement. Hank's eyes narrowed and his lips curled into a sneer as he stood up and shoved Buster.

"Now, if you is done, how's about we end this hunt? I've got a hankering for a drink and some of ya girl-friend's pussy."

Buster's laughter disappeared in an instant, his intense gaze fixed on Hank, his lips pressed tightly together, and his eyebrows creased in fury.

"You stay away from Josie, ya hear?"

Hank glared at him defiantly, his face contorted, his cheeks flushed with rage.

"Only if she stays away from me first."

With fury in his eyes, Buster tightened his grip on the shotgun, his face twisting into a snarl. Just as he was about to swing the butt of the shotgun at Hank, a distant thumping sound caught his attention, accompanied by a faint and desperate cry for help.

"You's a lucky sonofabitch," Buster growled as he turned toward the sound of the cry.

"I'm done leadin' the way. Get your ass into gear and let's end this."

With an angry grumble, Hank pulled himself to his feet and retrieved his rifle, wiping off stray leaves before crashing through the trees toward the continued sound of thumping.

Still filled with rage, Buster readjusted his grip on his shotgun and followed. Hank might be his little brother, but he would still need to be taught a lesson after this hunt was over.

Ahead of them, the forest fell eerily quiet. This was usually their favorite part, when their prey had given up trying to escape in favor of a last-ditch effort to hide instead. Hank looked over his shoulder and grinned at Buster. Despite the anger coursing through him, Buster's grin mirrored his brother's, their shared anticipation of the impending kill pushing aside any animosity.

Hank continued to follow the trail of blood, which led to a break in the trees. Stopping there, he scanned the area ahead and motioned for Buster to join him.

"There's some sort of building ahead. Looks like our man has got 'imself a refuge."

"Not for long," Buster said, shouldering past Hank and striding toward the building.

The structure on the opposite side of the clearing appeared aged but still sturdy. Branches from the nearby trees were scattered on the roof, and patches of moss grew on it, with the sun's rays emphasizing the vibrant greenish tint of the worn-out aluminium.

The building's appearance hinted at its past as a

factory, but given its isolated location in the woods, it could only imply a factory dedicated to producing one particular thing. Drugs. At least they hoped so.

The two brothers exchanged a knowing look and readied their weapons. They couldn't see any vehicles, but that didn't mean there weren't any concealed.

Buster took the lead and approached the door, the blood trail leading directly to it. The door was covered in bloody handprints, the doorknob slick with the sticky substance. Already in the heat of the day, flies were buzzing lazily around the entrance.

Buster nodded at Hank. The air was charged with anticipation as they both took cover on opposite sides of the door. With a grimace, he placed his hand on the bloody doorknob. He turned the knob and pushed the door inward, sprinting inside, his shotgun poised for action.

Startled by the unmistakable boom of a shotgun that wasn't his, Buster dove to the ground and scrambled for cover behind a nearby shelving unit. The unexpected clatter of a weapon falling to the floor behind him made him glance backward, and his eyes widened in shock.

Hank's pellet-ridden body was lying face down on the floor in a widening pool of blood, his weapon lying abandoned next to him.

"No!" Buster roared with fury. His breath came in short, ragged bursts as he stumbled to his feet, left his cover, and fired madly toward the source of the blast. He moved forward, firing his weapon in quick succession, leaving no opportunity for his enemy to retaliate without risking being blown away in the process.

"Wa... wait!" a trembling voice filled with fear called out.

"Ya killed ma brother and ya want me to wait?" Buster could feel the rage course through his veins as he sent another blast toward the hidden man.

Buster was close now. He rounded the corner of the lab table in front of him and saw the quivering form of a man wearing a lab coat and a shotgun lying on the floor next to him. Beside him was a body filled with pellets lying motionless in a pool of blood. It was the body of the man they had been hunting. One of the blasts Buster had unleashed had clearly found its mark.

Buster grinned, his sinister smile accentuated by the gaps where his teeth used to be, as the trembling figure on the ground locked eyes with him and let out a piercing scream of terror. The man scrambled backwards on all fours, leaped up, and rushed towards a door in the corner.

"Oh no ya don't," Buster said, raising his shotgun and taking aim before pulling the trigger, expecting to hear one last deafening bang, but all he got was a hollow click.

"Well, shit," he growled before throwing the useless gun aside. Bursting into the room, he saw the man struggling with the locked rear entrance door. The man, upon seeing Buster, dropped the keys and was scrambling to pick them up again when Buster shoulder tackled him, hurling him into the wall with a sharp crack. The man fell to the ground, motionless. Buster stared down at him, breathing hard, his anger barely contained.

"Time to make ya suffer, ya fucker." Buster's face broke out into a sinister smile, his eyes dripping with malice.

"Ha, that rhymes."

Despite his rage, Buster couldn't contain a laugh at his ingenuity as he picked up the man and threw him over his shoulder.

Present Day
River Mountain, Little Rock, AR

"C'mon in, don't be shy now," Buster said, his wide grin lighting up his face as he stood by the doorway, waving his hand to invite him inside.

"Thank you, sir," Jonas said, his eyes meeting Buster's briefly before looking away, with a shy, almost imperceptible nod as he brushed past Buster on his way in.

"Wyatt, your friend is here. Git your sorry ass down here," Buster called out, his voice thick with a country accent.

"Coming, Dad," Wyatt called back, his voice filled with annoyance.

"Is that fer us?" Buster said, pointing at the whiskey bottle in Jonas's hand.

"Oh yeah, sorry," Jonas said, his lips twitching nervously, and his jaw clenched with unease.

"What, ya think we rednecks or somethin' bringing us somethin' like that? What happened to good old wine?"

Buster stared at him, his eyebrows drawing together in a tight frown as he held out his hand for the bottle.

"Oh no sir, not at all. Sorry, I didn't mean to cause offense," Jonas said as he handed over the bottle with a trembling hand.

Buster stared at him a little longer, letting the awkward moment draw out before his face transformed into a wide grin.

"Ya should have seen ya face, I'm just fuckin' with ya." Buster said between loud guffaws as he slapped a palm on his thigh.

"Ya looked plain terrified, ya did."

He struggled to contain his laughter as he grabbed the bottle from Jonas's still-extended hand and walked away into the kitchen, shaking his head.

"Ya did just fine kid, we drink our whisky here as if it was water."

He returned from the kitchen to stand before Jonas, the corners of his eyes still crinkled with amusement.

As Jonas waited for Wyatt and his heart to stop racing, his eyes drifted to take in the house. The house was opulent and in immaculate condition, boasting an entryway adorned with a spotless golden-red rug. The rug led to a staircase with hand-carved wooden railings, polished to a sheen that he could have sworn he saw his reflection in. Paintings that looked like family portraits lined the wall leading upstairs. To his left was the entrance to a large open lounge area decorated with plush leather couches and a bar in the corner, rows of expensive-looking bottles littering the shelves behind the marble bench. To his right stood an expensive-looking dining table accompanied by matching chairs. Just beyond that was the kitchen. If there were a larger mismatch between occupants and the house itself, Jonas knew of none.

He stood there in awkward silence as Buster stared at him, a cheesy grin plastered on his face that didn't quite reach his eyes. As he tapped his foot anxiously, he could sense Buster's watchful eyes studying him intently. He could feel the anxiety building within him. Social anxiety had always had a hold over him, and Buster's unnerving gaze was only making it worse. He knew Wyatt's family had origins near the remote forest regions of the Ouachita National Forest before they struck it big, but he wasn't expecting them to have kept their redneck habits.

The minutes passed as the silence seemed to expand to envelop the entire house. A shiver ran down Jonas's spine, and he was on the verge of apologizing and leaving, when the heavy thud of Wyatt's footsteps echoed down the stairs.

Buster shifted his gaze toward Wyatt, his eyes fixed on the dirty tracks left behind by his boots. His eyes narrowed, a muscle pulsating in his clenched jaw as if he were struggling to contain an intense fury.

"Wyatt, take those darn godforsaken boots off right now. Can't ye see the tracks yer leavin'?"

Sure enough, Wyatt was leaving a trail of mud behind him as he trudged toward them.

"I just had to clean up after yer sorry ass when you came in. Now yer gonna disrespect me by doin' it again?"

Buster's face turned a furious shade of red as he forcefully grabbed Wyatt by the ear and twisted it, causing Wyatt to jerk his head to alleviate the pain.

"Now, listen here. Yer gonna clean that up right now, ya hear? An' if I ever see you doin' this again? Yer gonna catch a beatin' so hard, yer gonna piss blood fer a week."

Jonas stood dumbstruck as he took in the sight, his face turning ashen, before his brows knitted together in a slight frown of confusion at the sight of Wyatt's calm, goofy grin directed toward him.

"Yes dad. Sorry Dad," he said, his voice filled with mock sincerity.

"Good, now git," said Buster, releasing him with a forceful push.

He turned back to Jonas, all hints of his anger now gone, and flashed him a broad, cheerful smile.

"Well now, Wyatt will be back in jus' a minute. How's about we fix ya a drink?"

"Uh, no thanks, sir, I'm okay."

Jonas anxiously flicked his eyes between Buster and the departing Wyatt, his face still pale and ghostly.

Buster's smile stretched even wider, as if he was relishing Jonas's stunned expression in response to his and Wyatt's confrontation.

"I'm not taken' no for an answer. You's a guest in ma house, and I treat ma guest's right."

He stood silent for a few seconds, his unnerving smile still plastered on his face, his eyes fixed on Jonas before he turned and strode towards the fridge.

The sight of the rows of bottles in the open fridge caught Jonas's attention as Buster grabbed a pair. With practiced ease, Buster popped the tops open and handed a bottle to Jonas.

"Now, how's about I introduce ya to ma wife, Josie?"

"Josie, come git your pretty little ass down here. We's havin' a guest."

His voice boomed through the house, almost loud enough to shake the walls.

"Just ya wait a goddamn minute," a high-pitched angry voice called back from upstairs, "ya know I'm busy feedin' Junior."

"Fine then, take your goddamn time," Buster called back, his cheeks turning crimson as anger blazed in his eyes.

"Uh, it's okay, I'm happy to wait," Jonas reassured Buster, his gaze dropping to the floor, his hand trembling slightly as he took a nervous sip from his beer.

Buster stared at him with a stony gaze, every feature set in an unyielding, emotionless facade. Just as the silence was becoming almost too much to bear, Wyatt appeared again, a sheepish grin on his face, his eyes flickering between Jonas and Buster.

"Hey, where's mine?" He said, staring at the bottle in Jonas's hand.

"Git ya own damn beer," Buster said with a frown, his voice dripping with irritation as he turned and stalked toward the living room.

Wyatt laughed, his eyes sparkling with amusement. "Sorry about that. My dad has the worst anger issues. I don't know how my mum puts up with it."

He turned and headed toward the kitchen. "C'mon, let's catch up in here. My mum will be down soon, and we'll do the awkward introduction. Then I promise dinner will be a happier affair."

A sudden, thunderous thump shook the entire house, causing a cascade of plaster particles to fall from the ceiling, making Jonas jump in surprise. Jonas looked up with a wide-eyed stare, noticing multitudes of cracks lining the ceiling.

"Wha... What was that?" he said, taking deep breaths to calm himself and relax his tense muscles.

Wyatt's attempt to stifle his laughter failed at the sight of the bewildered expression on Jonas's face, erupting into a boisterous laugh reminiscent of his father's. In all the time he'd known him, Wyatt had always been stoic and rarely displayed any emotion. Right now, he was laughing uproariously, completely letting loose like never before.

"Don't worry, it's just my brother being a brat again," he said, regaining his composure, a wide smile still stretched across his face, his eyes glimmering with amusement.

"C'mon, I need to get myself that drink."

Wyatt retrieved a drink from the fridge and led the

way to the spotless marble kitchen table, with velvet cushioned chairs positioned around in perfect formation, pulling out a couple. The pair sat, already engaged in conversation.

Jonas had met Wyatt at senior school earlier that year; he had transferred there from a prodigious private school. Wyatt's cool presence under pressure and non-judgmental attitude had instantly drawn Jonas to him. Amidst a school culture of bullies and exclusive circles, it was a breath of fresh air to engage with someone who defied the norms and was easy to talk to.

When Jonas had questioned why Wyatt had left the private school in favour of an average public school, he said he'd grown tired of the uppity attitudes and privilege that ran riot there. He longed for genuine connections, not superficial friendships based on social status.

It wasn't long before they formed a strong friendship. This was the first time they had met outside of school after Wyatt had surprised him with a dinner invitation. He'd expected them to do something like go to the movies or the beach, but he agreed reluctantly. Jonas typically kept to himself, and he hadn't been to a friend's house for dinner before, so this was unfamiliar territory to him.

The longer the conversation went on, the more Jonas could feel the tension melting away from his body. He even found himself laughing a few times, his mood lightening considerably. Just as he was starting to feel at ease, Josie arrived with a wide grin, leaning against the door frame to observe the boys.

"Howdy, you must be Jonas," she said, holding out a hand in greeting.

"Oh... er... hi. Yes. I am, ma'am."

Scrambling to his feet, Jonas extended his hand and gave hers a gentle shake.

In her 40s and sporting a tattered-looking tank top and bleached blonde hair, she looked at least 10 years younger. Her features spoke of classical, timeless beauty —high cheekbones, manicured eyebrows, and immaculate makeup. Despite her ragged clothing, he couldn't help but feel attracted to her, which made him instantly uncomfortable. He was seventeen, and he was at his best friend's house, he reminded himself in disgust. He took a deep breath to regain his composure before his eyes fell upon a dark reddish patch on the lower left side of her tank top.

Just as he was about to ask what had happened, her expression gave him pause.

A stony look had settled on her face, her unreadable blue eyes hinting at something he couldn't understand. It was almost an exact match of the expression Buster had worn earlier.

"Oh, Mom, you got some of Junior's dinner on you again," Wyatt said with a sigh, shaking his head at her and letting out a chuckle.

"Oh, so I have," Josie replied, glancing down at the stain and then back at the boys, her wide smile reappearing, a faint reddish tinge to her cheeks betraying her embarrassment.

"I'll go get fixed right up. Then I'll get us some dinner goin'."

She turned and headed back up toward the stairs. "I hope you like stew," she called back over her shoulder.

"Mom makes the best stew, believe me," Wyatt said, shooting a grin at Jonas. "Come, help me set up the table."

A few minutes later, as the pair finished up, Josie appeared at the top of the stairs. Jonas froze at the sight of her, his jaw inadvertently dropping. Wearing a tight, form-fitting and low-cut black dress that ended above her knees, the dress showcased her ample assets and shapely thighs.

"She's a beauty, ain't she?" the playfully toned voice of Buster said to the side of him. Jonas nearly dropped his bottle. How the hell did a man that size move so quietly?

"Oh, er, sorry, I didn't mean to stare," Jonas said, his face turning beet red with embarrassment.

"Yeah, sure ye didn't," Buster said, his chuckle laced with menace, a sly smile playing on his lips as he locked eyes with Jonas.

With a slow, knowing smile spreading across her lips and a lingering gaze, Josie sashayed past him, accentuating her hip movements before disappearing into the kitchen.

Jonas could feel his anxiety skyrocketing, leaving him feeling physically drained. His experience thus far had not been what he'd expected at all, and he feared his behaviour would ruin his friendship with Wyatt. He needed to do better. In an attempt to ease his growing nervousness, he reassured himself that the weird vibe he sensed around Wyatt's parents was just a figment of his own anxious mind. His heart racing, he excused himself and asked Wyatt for directions to the bathroom and hurried there as fast as he could without drawing attention, trying to be inconspicuous. Closing the door behind him, he leaned against it and felt his heart pounding, as if it wanted to break free of his chest. Outside, he heard laughter and dishes clanging from the dining room as the table was lined with food.

In his panicked state, he couldn't shake the thought that the laughter was directed at him. From upstairs, the sound of loud thumping resumed, and he wondered if Junior was joining them for dinner at the table. His mind was racing in multiple directions, making it difficult to focus.

Closing his eyes, he took a few deep breaths, and as he splashed water over his face, he felt the stress slowly dissipate. He reassured himself that he just needed to get through dinner, and then he could leave. He just needed to hang on a bit longer. Nodding, he dried his face and returned to the dining room.

In his absence, the table had been adorned with a variety of small dishes. In the center, there was a beautifully arranged fruit platter that added a colorful touch to the occasion. A tempting spread of cheeses, dips, and savory biscuits awaited, meticulously arranged around it. A basket filled to the brim with small bread buns, their tops covered with a dusting of flour, and a small tub of freshly churned butter was within easy reach of everyone. Placed at the head of the table where Buster sat was a large metal bucket, filled with ice and an array of beer bottles. Jonas's whisky bottle he had brought as a gift sat next to it.

Wyatt had already taken his seat, his head down, looking at something on his phone when Jonas arrived. He looked up with a bored, almost reflexive grin, as if he was eager to return his focus to his phone.

"That's your seat there," he said, pointing at the seat next to him before redirecting his attention back to his phone.

"Thank you," Jonas said, taking the offered seat and casting a quick glance towards Buster, who acknowledged him with a grunt before shifting his focus back to his beer. Despite himself, Jonas could feel his heart rate climbing once again, and he began to wonder how he was going to make it through the dinner without having an anxiety attack.

With nothing else to do, Jonas took out his phone and began scrolling through his feed, desperate to try anything to distract himself. The scent of the stew drifting through the kitchen entrance was enough to punch through the nervous ball of energy in his gut, enticing hunger pangs to come crashing through in its stead.

"Here we are," Josie announced as she walked in, her oven mitt-covered hands wrapped around a large steaming stew pot, which she placed on a wooden serving board in the vacant spot on the table.

"Help yer selves," she said as she sat down in the seat next to Buster.

"Not you dear, you get the VIP treatment."

She directed a slow, deliberate smile toward Jonas, her eyes smouldering with intensity and locking onto his as she handed him a bowl already full of the steaming stew.

"Will Junior be joining us?" Jonas said, his cheeks flushing a deep shade of red, as he averted his gaze from her and focused instead on Wyatt and Buster, who were busy ladling steaming stew into their bowls.

"No, he's too annoying," Wyatt said with a snicker, which he stifled upon seeing Josie's tight-lipped glare.

"Junior has a few problems, which means he's gotta stay upstairs for a bit," Josie said, looking at Jonas with a warm smile.

"Plus, he's already had his dinner, which he was none too happy about. We've run out of 'is favourite food, which is why he's making such a racket up there," Buster added, his hand dipping into the chilled, ice-filled pail to retrieve a beer.

"We'll fix that right up soon," Buster continued quietly as he leaned back on his chair, twisting the top off of his beer, a subtle smirk forming at the corner of his mouth.

"Don't you want to ask something?" Wyatt said, giving Jonas a nudge.

"Oh yeah," Jonas said, his face turning a light shade of red.

"Um... Mr. Corbin, sir, may I ask about the history

of BioGenesis Solutions? I'm doing a school project about business success stories and would love to know about your company," Jonas said, struggling to look Buster in the eye.

Buster had just lifted his beer to his lips when he paused and stared at Jonas, his eyes narrowing, his face displaying a glimpse of irritation before settling on a neutral expression as he placed the bottle down.

"Eat first, and then I'll tell you what ya want to know," he said as he scooped up a piece of bread and plunged it into the stew before stuffing it into his mouth.

Jonas obediently took a few mouthfuls of stew. It was like no stew he'd had before. The meat's texture was curious—grainy and stringy, yet perfectly tender. The addition of Josie's spices infused it with flavor, making it more delicious than he had expected.

He noticed Josie staring at him intensely as he ate before she shifted her attention toward Buster. A broad smile spread across her face, exposing her slightly yellowed teeth, a contrast to her otherwise immaculate appearance. Buster returned her smile with one that mirrored her own.

Jonas finished the stew, his eyebrows furrowing in confusion. He glanced back and forth between them, attempting to unravel the silent exchange happening between them.

"Alright," Buster said, leaning back on his chair, his smile fading as he belched and rubbed his belly. "I'll tell ya tha' story. The actual story, not tha' one the public knows."

"What do you mean?" Jonas said, his eyebrows raised in surprise. "I thought it was the actual story?"

"Nah, the actual story is far more... unsavoury, I'm guessin' you could say," Buster said with a laugh before he leaned forward in his chair, his features hardening.

"I guess ya know how we was livin' just on the outskirts of the Ouachita National Forest? That part is the only proper part of the story."

He clenched his jaw as he recalled the events of that day.

"Ya see, me and me brother, we was hunters," he said, his eyes filled with intense focus as he stared at Jonas.

Without warning, Jonas was overcome with a sudden bout of nausea, causing his vision to blur and his body to tingle with an unsettling numbness. His panic level rose to new heights as he struggled to stand, but he couldn't even shift his legs. The weight of his arms felt like lead, immobilized on the table, unresponsive to any movement. No matter how hard he focused on them, he couldn't even lift so much as a finger.

"I... I can't move. What's... what's happening?" he whispered, his words strained and slurred as he fought to speak.

"Don't worry love, it's just a little something I put in your stew to relax ya a little," Josie said with a gentle smile, conveying a false sense of calm as she stood up from her chair and approached him, swaying her hips suggestively.

"Just relax. We's just about to have story time. It's what ya wanted, isn't it?" She shifted his chair to face her, and she sat down on his lap, her cleavage directly in his line of sight.

"Or is this what ya wanted?"

With a slight lean forward, she sensually brushed her lips over his neck, her fingers entwined in his hair.

Jonas could hear Wyatt's laughter next to him. "Enjoy bro, my mom has a great set. Everyone says so."

Josie laughed as she looked down, biting her lip, her eyes conveying a sense of longing as they focused on the bulge in his pants.

"Well, I can see that not everything is numb."

Terror filled Jonas's wide eyes, his facial muscles twitching, while Buster and Wyatt looked on, roaring with laughter.

Josie rose from his lap and moved his chair back to face Buster. Standing behind Jonas, she rested her hands on his shoulders, massaging them in a slow, sensual manner. She pulled his shoulders back slightly, allowing her breasts to rest against the back of his head.

"Now, as I was sayin'," Buster said, wiping away tears of laughter from his eyes. "Me and me brother was hunters, but we weren't ya typical hunters, no sir. What we hunted was humans."

As Buster continued his story, Jonas gaped at him in a silent scream, his eyes darting around the room in a desperate search for aid that wasn't there.

"We hunted them fer sport, ya see. Anyway, we was in the middle of a hunt in the forest when our prey went and found himself a warehouse. Can ye believe it? It was the middle of nowhere, we was in a part of the forest we never been before, and he just happened upon it. The luck, eh? We was huntin' dozens of times before this, but we ain't ever found it."

After taking a final swig of his beer, he resumed his story.

"The guy got in and we followed 'is trail to the door. We forced our way inside. My brother, he..." Buster's eyes darkened as his fury rose.

"My brother got blasted by a shotgun and went down. I dove to save meself. I was mad with anger and started blastin' back at the fella who'd got me brother. He never had a chance to fire back, and I found 'im there cowerin' behind a table. Our prey was layin' next to him. One of my blasts had got 'im."

Buster extended his hand towards the bucket holding the beer, but then he paused and changed course to grab the bottle of whisky. Grabbing a nearby glass, he dropped a few ice cubes from the bucket into it and poured himself a drink. In one fluid motion, he lifted the glass to his mouth and drank it in one gulp. Wiping his lips, he poured himself another.

"Hmm... not bad," he said, elevating the glass to eye level and giving the whisky inside a gentle swirl.

"I wasn't about to let the bastard get away with killin' me brother. So, I tied 'im up and tortured 'im. Long story short, he spilled the beans on 'is little operation so he could save 'is sorry ass. The next part is the reason why we're rich and why you're here. I'm sure you're dyin' to find out." He chuckled obscenely before he readied two other glasses, dropping in some ice and filling them with whisky before handing them to Josie and Wyatt. After a sip, they smiled at Buster and motioned for him to continue.

"Now, turns out this guy was a scientist. Michael 'is name was. He was a whizz at plant life. He'd discovered a new fungus growing in the national forest and was doin' experiments with it on animals he'd captured. Ya should have seen the cages filled with 'em at the back of the place. Some nasty things those were, 'specially after what the fungus did to 'em. Ya see, the fungus made them grow into somethin' different. They weren't animals no more; they was some sort of hybrid. Some turned into great pulsin' lumps of flesh, others grew lots of arms and legs, some didn't work well with the stuff and just exploded. The ones that didn't though, they all had one thing in common. They grew to at least double their original size, and they was tasty. Our scientist had found a way to increase our food supply, turnin' what couldn't be eaten into things that could. As a bonus, the meat also slowed down the agin' process. It changed the bodies of those who ate it somehow, but not in a way that could be seen. To cut the story short, I forced 'im to teach me how it worked, what to do to make the mixture, then I killed 'im and decided to turn it into a business. Now we sell's the meat everywhere and no one's the wiser as to what it is or where it came from. We's cuts it to look like any other meat ya see, and it smells the same. Just has an extra tang of flavor which we're famous for. Fair payment, I'd say in return fer losin' me brother."

"Wh... Wh... Why..." Jonas struggled to form words, his voice barely above a whisper.

"Let me guess, you're askin' why you're here and what you've got to do with it?"

"Well, here's the thing, Jonas ma boy. Ya see, just before 'e died, Michael was pleadin' and blabbin' about havin' a brother, a son, a wife and whatnot, so's to try and get sympathy, hopin' that I'd let him live. That didn' work out so well for 'im. But he did say his son's name was Jonas. Now imagine my surprise when Wyatt mentioned 'e'd made a new friend at school named Jonas whose daddy had died ten years ago and happened to be a scientist who lived in Arkansas."

Jonas struggled to speak and move, his panic overwhelming him. He fought to regain control of his limbs, straining to bring life back into his arms and legs. With relief, he felt a gentle tingling sensation in his fingers and toes, a welcome sign of returning feeling. Standing up, Buster refilled the three glasses with whisky, and without hesitation, the three family members all downed their drinks in a single, synchronized gulp.

"Whoa, this stuff is going straight to ma head," Buster said, his eyebrows furrowing in concentration as he wobbled slightly, gripping onto the table to steady himself.

"So, sweetie, you just happened to come along at the right time," Josie said, taking over from Buster and casting a concerned glance toward him.

"Our Junior was born with some difficulties, maybe a side effect of the enhanced meat. Since he was a babe, he would only ever eat meat, and only the enhanced stuff. But the meat he wanted wasn' from just any animal. It was human. Human meat enhanced with our BioGen mix. We tried giving him other meat, but he wouldn't stop whoopin' and hollerin', so we grabbed a homeless fella livin' on the streets in the city, gave him some BioGen and watched him grow. That man ballooned to three times he's size, I swear on my soul." She giggled, a dreamy look in her eyes.

"Anyway, we cut 'im up and found our Junior stopped complainin'. Ever since then, we been grabbing people that wouldn't be missed. Satisfies Buster too, he missed his huntin'," she looked at Buster, her eyes filled with warmth before widening in alarm.

"Honey, what's wrong?"

"I... I just need to sit for a bit," Buster said, slumping back down in his chair, his head in his hands.

"Keep goin'. We need our meat as tasty as possible."

With a frown, Josie blinked and shook her head, as if trying to shake off the foggy effects of the alcohol herself.

"Well, we ran out of our last fella a few days ago now. So, we decided to kill two birds with one stone, get Wyatt to invite ya over and use ya as Junior's next meal for the next few months or so dependin' on how big you grow after your injection and how worked up we got ya. Ya see, we found that the more we work our victim up, the more the juices are flowin', the tastier and more fillin' the meat. As for the explanation of you goin' missing, we'll just say you never made it to our house. Of course, Wyatt will be missin' his friend, but sacrifices must be made. For your brother, right Wyatt?"

Josie directed her gaze at Wyatt, whose head was lolling, slumped in his chair, his eyes closed.

"Wyatt?" With shaky steps, Josie approached him, extending her hand to shake his shoulder but failing as she crumbled to the floor with a groan.

"Okay, you can come in now," Jonas mumbled into his chest.

"Wait... what the fuck you mean by that?" Buster said, struggling to rise from his seat, his head drooping in exhaustion.

The front door burst open, serving as Buster's answer. A man in full riot gear, his face obscured by a helmet, stepped through the doorway and advanced toward the table, his gun trained on Buster.

"He means this," the man said, lifting his visor on his riot helmet. "You did well, son. I'm proud of you," he said, clapping a hand onto Jonas's shoulder.

"Let me introduce myself. I'm Nick, Michael's brother, and I've been waiting for this moment for ten years, you sonofabitch." His face contorted with a blend of hatred, pain, and disgust as he directed his words towards Buster.

"It looks like that whisky with a little added something did the trick," Nick said with a grin as he surveyed the three members of the Corbin family.

Buster gritted his teeth and with one final burst of effort screamed, "Junior, ya momma's in trouble, help!"

before he slumped back in his chair, his head hanging listlessly.

A sudden inhuman screeching and wailing from above sent chills down Jonas's spine as Nick whirled around and aimed his gun towards the roof. The house trembled as loud thuds reverberated on the ceiling above them, causing large cracks to form in the plaster.

The air filled with a dusty haze as chunks of plaster fell to the floor. Jonas gasped in shock, his mouth agape, as enormous, slippery tentacles burst through the gaps in the ceiling. They writhed and thrashed in a furious rage, their movements a blur as they whipped from one corner of the room to the other, a terrifying whirlwind of destruction searching for a victim.

With a rough shove, Nick toppled over the chair Jonas was sitting on, throwing himself down next to him and firing a few rounds at the tentacles, hoping for a lucky shot. A tentacle struck his gun and sent it wide just as he fired, and a crimson plume of blood erupted from Josie's prone form as one of his bullets struck her in the head, sending it snapping back with sickening force.

As the tentacles continued to whip around in rage, one of them found the slumped over Wyatt and wrapped itself around him. Fuelled by rage, the monster, unable to see its victim, retracted its tentacle before unleashing it with the force of a battering ram, slamming Wyatt into one wall, then another, with bone-jarring crunches that echoed through the room. Wyatt's body, bent and broken into impossible angles, rose up through the hole in the roof as the tentacle retreated. A howl of anguish reverberated through the house when the creature above saw the broken body of its brother.

Cracks, like spiderwebs, spread across the weakened ceiling from the holes, as the house groaned under the weight of the furious monstrosity.

"Fuck. I've got to get you out of here," Nick said, lifting Jonus up and placing his arm over his own shoulder for support. "Can you walk?"

"I... I think so."

Together, the two made their way toward the front door, Jonas dragging his feet, unable to put any weight on them. Nick led Jonas toward his Ford Explorer, opening the passenger side door and guiding him inside.

As he turned back around to face the house, a thunderous crash reached his ears, and a wave of dust and plaster plumed from the open front door. The upper floor of the house had collapsed, sending the tentacled thing to the ground and, judging by the weak keening noises he heard, crushing Buster and his wife.

"I've got to go and take care of this. I'll be back. Don't you worry, okay?" he said with a glance at Jonas.

Jonas could only manage a weak nod in response before Nick rushed off towards the rear of his vehicle, popping the boot to retrieve something from the inside.

His vision faded in and out as he watched Nick run toward and inside the house, a small cylindrical object clutched in one hand.

A few moments later, a tremendous boom shook the house. The windows erupted in a fiery explosion, sending shattered glass, debris, and chunks of grey matter hurtling onto the lawn.

"N... Nick."

A mixture of sobs and gasps escaped Jonas's lips as he struggled to slide out of the passenger side door only to collapse on the ground, his legs unable to bear his weight.

Tears streamed freely down his cheeks as he buried his face in his hands. Not only had he lost his dad to the Corbin's, now he'd lost Nick too. An overwhelming feeling of loss and defeat came over him. What was the point of doing all this if the bastards had won in the end, destroying what little family he had left?

"Hey, you're not getting rid of me that easily, kiddo," Nick said, emerging through the smoke, his face beaming with a grin. "Now, let's get you to the hospital. I hear they've improved the quality of food there. You might even get some ice cream."

A wave of laughter overcame Jonas, a turbulent blend of relief, anxiety, and the lingering trauma of the night's events. Nick's strong arms encircled him, lifting him to his feet. Overwhelmed by a torrent of emotions, his body shook violently as Nick held him close. Over Nick's shoulder, Jonas could see the flames licking at the walls of the house, the beginnings of the blazing inferno it would soon become. It was finally over.

Behind them, unseen through the haze of smoke and embers, the severed end of a tentacle writhed weakly as it pulled itself along the ground toward safety. Awareness, raw and primitive, bloomed inside its tissues as it dragged itself under a nearby bush. Someday soon, it would be whole again.

Mind Games

Jax, the alien, nonchalantly walked out of the President's Oval Office, leaving behind a fiery explosion. The alien had the classic appearance of the grey-skinned figures regularly portrayed in films, TV, and documentaries. It had a slender body, elongated fingers and toes, and a large oval-shaped head with two large, lightly protruding black eyes. With a grin on its face, Jax looked directly into the camera, giving a wink to Blake before the words "Game Over" flashed on the TV screen and the credits rolled.

Blake leaned back with a satisfied smile, placing his controller on the table, savoring the credit music, and relishing the post-game cooldown after the intense final mission.

The game he had just finished playing was called *Humanity's Destruction*, and it was currently the hottest video game out there. It had been released two weeks ago with a massive marketing budget, and lately, it had been the only thing the kids at school were talking about. Most of his friends had been playing it too, and he had enjoyed chatting with them about where they were up to in the game as the days went by.

Even though his peers saw him as a geek, 16-year-old Blake's intelligence and knack for witty comebacks won over the jocks who tried to bully him, making him surprisingly popular. As such, he was continually getting messages from the jocks, geeks, and everyone in between, so his phone was constantly dinging with the sound of messages.

The sound of one such familiar ding caught Blake's attention as he picked up his phone and saw a message pop up on the screen. It was from his best friend, Matt.

> Dude, I just finished Humanity's Destruction. That ending though

Blake was on the verge of replying when the house abruptly shook as if a colossal earthquake had begun directly beneath his home. Except...the source wasn't below the ground. It seemed to be coming from above the roof.

Under the pressure of a powerful external force, the timbers of the house groaned and creaked, while a dazzling light poured through the windows of the living room where Blake was seated on the couch. Blake slid off and huddled on the floor, terrified that the roof would collapse on top of him, shielding his eyes from the blinding light.

Just as he thought the house was about to crumble,

the shaking stopped, and the light vanished, leaving small plaster pieces scattered on the floor and particles gently descending from the ceiling as the sole proof of what had occurred.

While the house had stopped shaking, his body continued to tremble. In an effort to calm himself down, he focused on his breathing and gradually uncurled his body from the defensive position he had assumed to safeguard against potential falling debris.

Standing up gingerly, he remained in position for a couple of minutes, ensuring it was secure before exploring. There was absolute silence, as if nothing had happened, not even a single creak of floorboards or a groan of timber.

With a sense of bewilderment, Blake approached the front door and cautiously cracked it open to see what was happening outside. A cool night breeze swept in, bringing relief to the nervous heat his body was generating. Pushing the door open further, he leaned out and scanned the surroundings. Complete darkness. There wasn't a single streetlamp that was lit, and all the houses in the neighborhood seemed to have suffered a power loss, just like his. The only source of light was the dim moonlight that filtered through the clouds, casting dim shadows on the ground from the houses and trees.

He was about to close the door when he caught the sound of his name being called from the street. It sounded like his mom.

Blake paused. His parents were out watching a movie and weren't due back for another hour. Even if they were back, why would they be standing out in the middle of the street? It made no sense.

"Blake, come here, darling," the voice called out again. The voice was strange, lacking any trace of his mom's familiar tone.

For a fleeting moment, a distant flash of lightning unveiled something clearly impossible. Blake's heart raced as he swiftly shut and locked the door, leaning against it for support.

Fear began to course through him as the doorknob rattled behind him at an impossible speed, then abruptly ceased as quickly as it began. Silence once again regained its throne as the lightning outside continued to send bursts of light through the windows, casting unsettling shadows on the floor.

Blake turned around cautiously and spent a couple of minutes with his ear pressed against the door, ensuring that the potential intruder had left, before sinking to the floor, his back firmly against it. Was he hallucinating? Maybe the game had subconsciously influenced him, unnerving him to the point where his mind was playing tricks on him. He didn't think so though; he had felt nothing but satisfaction at the completion of the game, and he hadn't found playing it scary at all.

The rattling of the doorknob once again shattered the silence, this time slower and more deliberate, accompanied by the sound of the door unlocking.

"Mom? Dad? Is that you?" he called out in relief. Maybe it was them after all. Maybe he had imagined what he had seen and heard outside after all.

The doorknob turned, and the door was pushed inward gently, as if to signal that it was alright for him to welcome them inside.

"It's us, honey, let us in."

Blake's overwhelming sense of relief made him oblivious to the unusual tone of his mom's voice beyond the door. He stood up and cleared the path for the door to open behind him. What was behind was definitely not his mom or his dad. It was Jax.

Overwhelmed by shock, Blake crumpled to the floor, his eyes locked on Jax as darkness engulfed him.

A sharp, searing pain behind his eyes awoke Blake, prompting him to sit up immediately, opening his eyes to a room filled with blinding light. He was lying on a flat table; the lights combined with the surgical appearance of the table and the absence of any other furniture almost made him feel like he was in an operating theatre. Tears streamed down his face as he blinked frantically, struggling to adjust to the bright light, when a loud voice suddenly startled him from somewhere in the room. It took a few moments before he understood. The voice didn't come from within the room; it was invading his mind directly with a jarring and unnatural force, an alien energy that felt wholly aggressive.

Turn around, the voice said. Its tone lacked anything resembling empathy, warmth, or humanity.

To his dismay, Blake's body was utterly submissive to

the voice's instructions, offering no resistance. A sharp pain shot like lightning down from his forehead when he thought about trying to, causing his limbs to spasm as if he were being electrocuted.

He slid off the table and mechanically twisted his legs around, the rest of his body compelled to follow as it turned in the direction the voice commanded.

Standing before him was Jax. He resembled the video game character in every conceivable way, as impossible as it seemed. Other than the table Blake had been lying on, the room was effectively empty. The presence of panels embedded in every surface filled the room with bright white light, erasing any shadows from the two figures and the table.

Blake's vision blurred once more, signalling another impending collapse as a jolting pain coursed through his head, locking his limbs in position. Every attempt to move proved futile. No part of his body, not even his eyes, could shift away from Jax.

I will talk, and you will listen. We have been studying you, not just because of your interest and involvement in the avatar simulation, but because you possess all the qualities required for the upcoming role you will assume.

With that, the wall beside Jax flickered as a scene came into view. From an overhead camera angle, a building in ruins was visible, and smoke was billowing out. Blake's horrified gasp was prompted by the slow zooming out of the camera, as he finally understood what he was seeing.

It was the White House, or what was left of it. Its

destruction was virtually complete with only a few walls still standing. The rest of the building lay in ruins, while the surrounding land was left completely untouched. The White House had clearly been struck by a weapon that surpassed any earthly weapon in precision.

Blake's mind was seized by a sudden realization—it felt like the game *Humanity's Destruction* had sprung to life. Surely, this couldn't be real.

Your avatar simulation gave us useful information. We captured the creator of the simulation and forced him to insert a method to capture data from the users of the simulation so we could determine who would be the most useful to us. The one who would aid in controlling your race on our behalf. Through your voice, we will ensure that humans follow the directions we give you. You will be our avatar; we will be your controller. You will be what your people call, the President, and with our direction, along with technology and instructions embedded in your voice and transmitted to the world from the implant in your brain, the world will be shaped to our liking. Our slaves for eternity or until we tire of our toy.

Blake wanted to scream in horror but could utter no sound. He wanted to cry but could produce no tears. He wanted to surrender to darkness and release his mind, but it refused to allow him to. No matter what he tried, he just stood there. Silent. A puppet, now totally under the puppeteer's control. His face contorted into a forced smile as peals of laughter tore from his throat, a chorus of alien laughter joining in while deep inside the recesses of his mind, he screamed.

MASKED RAGE

As they drifted in their boat off Isla del Cano, an island off the coast of Costa Rica, Harry, his wife Mary, and their two sons, Jake who was eighteen and Henry thirteen, took in the salty breeze and the sound of seagulls overhead.

Harry had been planning this holiday for months now, and it was one he sorely needed. The so-called nine-to-five job of running a mechanic's shop had become a relentless endeavor, leaving him feeling worn out, irritable, and thoroughly miserable by the time he returned home after 8 pm each night. That was even more irritable and miserable than he usually was.

On top of that, he had to deal with his family. First it was Mary asking about his day and talking about hers. Then there was Henry, perpetually whining and crying about his schoolwork or the latest spat with his friends. And Jake, who was always on the phone with his girlfriend. The noise in the house was relentless—a stark contrast to what he longed for after a day of dealing with ungrateful customers and incompetent employees. Over time, he had grown resentful of the lot of them. The least they could do was show gratitude to him for providing for them. At least Mary expressed her appreciation in the bedroom. That thought brought a fleeting smirk to his face.

Harry was not a nice man. His employees, his family, and even he himself was aware of it, but rather than feeling ashamed, he felt a sense of satisfaction. After all, if he were considerate, he wouldn't have the somewhat luxurious lifestyle he enjoyed now. Harry took opportunities when they arose with cold precision, and if they didn't come, he made them himself. Though ruthless in his business dealings, he was renowned for his ability to get things done efficiently, which came at the cost of his local suppliers, who were desperate for his business and ended up having to cut their profits.

Harry put aside his musings as he zipped up his snug wetsuit and hefted the weight of the oxygen tank onto his shoulders, securing the straps.

"Last chance, no skin off my nose if you don't come," Harry stated to his family coolly as he grabbed the diving mask off the leather seat overlooking the vast ocean before them.

He glared at his family with narrowed eyes filled with disdain, his lips curled in a sneer as they all looked away from him, avoiding his gaze.

"Ungrateful, the lot of you," he snarled, nostrils

flaring as he turned his back on them to sit on the edge of the boat, his back facing the water.

Mary, Jake, and Henry had shown excitement when he announced the holiday, but their enthusiasm rapidly faded when they realized it was another of Harry's self-serving endeavors. Ignoring their wishes, he unapologetically structured the itinerary entirely around his own preferences. As far as he was concerned, his family should be grateful just to be with him for this holiday. It's not like everyone had the same chance to visit these places as he had given them.

With one last piercing glare at each of them, he secured the mask over his face, the smell of rubber filling his nostrils, and fell backward into the water.

He hung stationary in the water just below the surface as he waited for his senses to acclimatize. At this depth, the water shimmered with a brilliant blue hue, as if reflecting the sky above. Sunlight penetrated the surface, casting ethereal rays that illuminated floating particles. Small fish moved speedily, their movements purposeful as they searched for remnants of food.

The anger that had consumed Harry melted away as he took in the breathtaking sights of the underwater world. In the distance, a school of tuna caught his eye, while a couple of inquisitive sea turtles altered their course to swim closer, maintaining a cautious distance but stretching their necks to get a better look at him. Below him, he spotted a couple of moray eels, their gently swaying heads poking out from the coral and rocks where they were hiding. Where he was, the depth of the ocean floor was roughly sixteen feet, a perfect starting point for his dive.

Swimming downward, he made his way along the sloping reef. Flashes of movement came from the reef below as startled fish darted away, their scales reflecting in the fading light as they disappeared into the distance. Nearby, puffs of silt exploded as an octopus in camouflage retreated, its tentacles propelling it to safety. Ahead of him, a large ray gracefully glided through the water, unperturbed by Harry's presence.

Harry felt a soothing calm wash over him, a stark contrast to the fiery anger that usually consumed him. There was something about the sea that calmed him. Since he had started diving with his family as a child, it always had. It was such a vast space, full of sea life that acted on instinct and not emotion, beings after his own heart.

As he explored deeper, the once brilliantly blue surroundings grew darker, enveloping him in a deep blue ambiance. Eyeing him curiously, a pod of dolphins swam close by, doing a few laps around him before shooting up to the surface. As they jumped into the air, a burst of light appeared as they broke the waterline before they splashed back down, putting on an acrobatic display for anyone lucky enough to witness it.

The brief light provided by their antics was enough to reveal a deep crevice in the ocean floor below him. It looked to be an aftereffect of a recent earthquake, evident from the broken coral that remained scattered but alive in the vicinity.

Intrigued, he decided to swim down and take a closer look. To his surprise, the crack in the ocean floor was wide enough for him to pass through. Looking into the opening, he noticed it seemed to connect to a cavern. The rock walls within extended and disappeared down into a pitch-black darkness.

Aiming the beam from the light strapped to his wrist, he peered into the depths of the rift. It revealed nothing but a large empty cavern that seemed curiously devoid of any sea life.

With caution, he swam through the gap, mindful of the rough, jagged rocks that threatened to scrape against his body on either side. With only the light from his wrist-mounted flashlight, the surroundings seemed even darker and more mysterious. Here, the water had a denser quality, and he could make out silt particles floating, frozen in place. The absence of a current added an eerie touch to his surroundings, putting him on edge. He decided to explore further, and with each stroke, he felt the water getting colder as he descended to the bottom. The ocean floor was adorned with rocks and scuttling crabs, creating a lively scene below. Suddenly, a glimmer in the distance caught his attention, its brilliance amplified by the stream of light from his wrist.

Beneath his mask, his eyes widened in surprise as he drew closer to the bottom of the ocean floor. An ancient-looking coin was the source of the glimmer. There was some kind of symbol on it, but he wouldn't be able to examine it properly until he got to the surface. He grabbed it, used his flashlight to scan the surroundings, and then halted, astonished by the sight in front of him. Before him stood a pillar crafted from stone and adorned with carvings, while scattered coins, similar to the one he had just picked up, were strewn about the surrounding area. There were stone blocks that had broken off from a wall, which he could glimpse just beyond the pillar lying nearby. As he got closer, he noticed the wall seemed to converge together to create a curved entrance. It was a temple, its ancient walls standing tall and proud, filled with the whispers of history. A surge of excitement coursed through his veins as he imagined the wealth that awaited him. Eager to see what treasure awaited him inside, he swam toward the opening, his heart pounding in his chest. The hissing of his oxygen tank reminded him to try and calm down. *Gotta save that air* he thought. The idea of dying down here was something he did not even want to comprehend.

Upon entering, he was immediately struck by the walls, which were covered with an endless array of carefully etched symbols.

A meticulously carved depiction of a mask dominated the center wall at the back, demanding attention. Despite being submerged for centuries, the intricate carvings in the temple remained extraordinarily sharp and vibrant. The beam from his torch revealed a pattern of smaller masks lining the walls and pillars, mirroring the larger one.

Returning his attention to the giant mask, he moved closer, captivated by its imposing presence, and studied its every feature. The stonework was flawless. The stone from which it was carved had a black, glasslike appearance, reflecting the torchlight off the mask's subtly raised features. Among them, there was one that stood out and caught his attention. The right eye was raised higher than the left eye. Frowning, he moved toward it, running his hand over it. With a shudder, the mask yielded to the pressure of his touch, sinking inward. A resonating sound of a muffled, explosive crack filled the temple, followed by the distinct rumble of heavy stone moving as a hidden doorway appeared beside the mask.

The revealing of the entrance had Harry so mesmerized that he was oblivious to a loose pillar breaking away from the roof, a result of the stone shifting for the first time in centuries. Startled, he propelled himself backwards as chunks of stone crashed to the floor with dull, echoing thuds. The temple trembled as its weakened supports struggled to bear the weight of the shifting structure and the force of water rushing in through the newly opened entrance.

With the temple still trembling, Harry swam toward the exit, his heart pounding as the water around him rippled violently with each tremor. To his relief, the temple seemed to stabilize after a few minutes, evoking one last protesting groan and stone fragment shower before settling.

Taking a long, deep breath to calm his pounding heart, Harry advanced towards the uncovered door. As he glimpsed the ominous darkness ahead, a sense of trepidation washed over him, a shiver shooting down his spine. Down here, darkness hit harder than it did anywhere else. It didn't help that there had been no sign of sea-life since he'd started investigating in the temple. He entered and scanned the area with his flashlight, his hands trembling. Much to his astonishment, there appeared to be a gap above without water, indicating an air pocket. As he moved toward the lip of the wall, he could feel the anticipation building inside him. He broke through the surface and with one smooth motion, lifted the mask off his head, eager to take in the marvels that awaited him in this chamber. As he swept his arm around the room, his eyes widened in amazement at the sheer beauty that surrounded him.

The chamber, constructed wholly of the mask carving's black glasslike stone, emitted a mysterious aura with the light reflecting off the walls, giving the room a mystical, dark purplish glow. Before him, a series of small steps spiraled upward, leading to a pedestal. Dangling from a partly intact stand on the pedestal was a mask that appeared surprisingly well-preserved, as if someone had crafted it a year ago instead of thousands of years ago. The mask seemed to be made from the glasslike material that he had become familiar with. Fragments of the rest of the stand littered the base of the pedestal, likely a result of the recent temple tremors.

The longer Harry studied the mask, the more he found himself unable to look away from it. In fact, he didn't want to. He had found the mask after all, and it was his for the taking. The archaeologists could have the rest of the temple, history be damned. Without even touching it yet, it felt like the mask was a part of him already, as if it had always belonged in his world. As familiar to him as his family, his business, his home.

Without thinking, he hoisted himself up from the ledge and moved towards the pedestal, his unwavering gaze locked onto the mask. The closer he got, the more the chamber seemed to come alive with faint whispers, the mask's glow becoming more pronounced under the torchlight Harry aimed at it, but his single-minded desire for the mask prevented him from hearing or seeing anything else.

His hands trembled with hunger as he reached for the mask, fingertips grazing its smooth surface. He traced the intricate patterns with reverent care, each curl and notch whispering something nameless. Around him, the air thickened with voices—urgent, layered, impossible to ignore. Images of a tantalizing alternate reality danced through his mind, urging him to succumb to the mask's power and embrace his hidden desires. He would be revered and celebrated, known for his power and commanding both fear and respect. Power, yes, that is what he wanted most in life—the power for him to speak and have people do things without question, without protest. Anyone who resisted would be made an example of. A lesson for those who would dare defy him.

He could no longer resist. With reverence, he lifted the mask and positioned it over his face. As it settled on him, a surge of power coursed through his veins. Every buried desire sharpened into purpose, and in that instant, he was no longer merely himself. He was whole. The mask clung to his face, adapting and conforming to his every contour, whispering promises of world-altering potential if he surrendered himself fully to its influence. He felt the last natural resistance to the foreign object fade away, and he smiled. Two had now become one.

Rage consumed his being as memories of all the people who had defied him raced through his mind like a slideshow. Chief among them was his family. How dare they question and talk back to him? A blazing flame of pure white-hot anger consumed his mind, and he knew exactly what needed to be done.

Mary stared into the sea, her face creased with tension, awaiting Harry's return. He had been gone sometime now, and she expected him back any moment, fixing them with an angry glare, the greeting she and her two sons had become accustomed to.

For months now, Mary had been intending to leave him, but she couldn't bring herself to do it, even with her friends' encouragement and support. She felt that at her age, no one would find her attractive and she would be alone forever. However, this trip had been the last straw. She had finally decided to end the relationship once they arrived on land. She knew that once she broke the news to Harry, she would have to travel back home with her sons, pack their things, and make their escape before he returned from his holiday lest they face his wrath. It was only a few days ago that the bruises from his last outburst had faded, and she wasn't going to let him lay his hands on her again. Over her dead body.

As Mary's gaze fell upon Jake and Henry, her heart sank at the sadness and anger etched on their faces, their slumped bodies speaking volumes. They didn't want to be here. They didn't want to spend time with their dad. They had complained so many times to her over the past few years and urged her to leave him and take them with her, but she had stayed, convincing herself that it was for the best if they all stayed together, despite knowing better.

No more. They would leave, move in with her parents for a while until she found another place, get her son's some help so they could work through the damage done to them by their father, and life would finally be something to look forward to again.

As she scanned the sea, she spotted a figure in the distance flailing their arms trying to catch her eye and get her attention. As they drew closer, she could see it was a man in a coast guard boat. He pulled up a few meters away from their craft, offering her a smile.

"Hello," he called out, his voice warm and friendly.

"Hello," Mary responded, her lips curved upward in a thin, stiff smile.

"How are you folks doing? Are you out here on holiday?"

"That's right," she called out, her tone short and sharp, trying to convey disinterest so the man would move on.

"Are you planning on doing any diving today? If you

are, I just need to check your permits to make sure you're authorized."

"Oh, uh, we're not, but my husband is already on a dive."

"I see. Can I see your permit?"

"Um... I'm not sure where it is. He should be back any minute, though. Are you able to wait until he returns?"

"Sure, madam, I'll just check in with the office."

In that moment, the calm water erupted as Harry burst through the surface, catching everyone by surprise. He moved towards the rear of the boat and pulled himself up with a disconcerting mechanical grace.

"Honey, when you're ready, this lovely coast guard is asking for your dive permit."

Her panicked eyes met his and darted away again to the coast guard, but his expression remained hidden behind the dive mask as he stood there motionless. A sense of unease washed over her. His presence felt off somehow, as if she were staring at a stranger.

In complete silence, he ripped off his mask, and Mary's horrified scream filled the air when she witnessed what lay hidden beneath.

"Harry, what's happened to your face?" she shrieked, stepping backwards, her eyes wide with fear.

Staring at her, his cheeks crimson with fury, Harry's eyes shone ominously through the glittering black surface of the mask. It had fused to his face so seamlessly that it was difficult to discern where the mask ended and his features began. Skin had grown around the mask as if the two had melded together, creating an unholy union. A smile formed, his lips curling back and revealing his teeth, which were now blackened and appeared to be crafted from the same material as the mask.

"Sir, are you alright?" the man from the coast guard called out with genuine concern, noticing Mary's startled reaction.

The smile on Harry's face faded as he turned toward him.

"So, you called the coast guard on me, did you, Mary?" he said, turning back to her, his voice deep and guttural, no longer recognisable as his own.

"N...No," she stammered, her voice filled with fear as she moved herself in front of her sons. She took a step back, her body rigid, as she assured him, "He was simply doing his routine patrol and wanted to stop by and make sure everything was okay."

Harry let out a deep, exasperated sigh. "Oh, Mary, lying again, I see. You know, I'm so sick of hearing your lies, excuses, and whining," he said as he stepped forward menacingly, his jaw clenched with rage.

"I think it's time to fix that. You will serve as an example of what will happen to those who question, lie, and complain to me, so that no one ever does it again."

With an intimidating stride, he approached, his presence looming over her like a dark cloud.

"I deserve respect. I deserve to be obeyed. I deserve happiness, and you are getting in the way of that."

With a surge of adrenaline, Mary instinctively shoved Jake and Henry to safety as Harry grabbed hold of her shirt and effortlessly lifted her off the deck. "Dad! No! Let her go!" Jake cried as he rushed forward to help her.

"Get away, you little brat," Harry snarled as he grabbed him with his other hand and hurled him against the side of the boat with a loud thud.

"No!" Mary screamed, struggling hopelessly to get to Jake.

"Sir, put her down. Now," the coast guard called out. From the corner of her eye, Mary noticed he had pulled out a gun and aimed it at Harry.

"No, I don't think I will," Harry growled, as he slammed Mary with all his might into the railing. The sound of crunching bones filled the air as her spine snapped and she fell motionless to the floor of the boat. Every now and then her body would spasm like a fish flipping about for its last breath.

"Mom?" Jake said weakly, his eyes fluttering as blood trickled down his forehead, blurring his vision, while Henry stood frozen in the cabin doorway, screaming in shock.

In an instant, the sharp crack of a gunshot filled the air, but Harry barely flinched as the bullet struck him, the power of the mask flooding through him as his body absorbed the impact with a dull thud. Without hesitation, he spun around, ready to launch himself off the boat toward the coast guard. More gunshots rang out, and bullets pounded into his body, yet he remained undeterred.

Just as he was about to leap, Jake used the last ounce of his strength to lunge at Harry, delivering a powerful blow. Not yet fully assimilated, the mask's grip on Harry loosened as Jake's strike connected with the side of his head. Jake collapsed onto the deck, exhausted. Harry stumbled, momentarily disoriented, as more gunshots found their mark, finally breaching his defenses. Stumbling toward the boat's side, he lost his balance and tumbled over the railing. A crimson stain spread across the water's surface as his body, still and lifeless, sank below.

Mary's eyes fluttered open; she saw Jake crawling toward her, while Henry trembled nearby in terror, continuing to scream as tears streamed down his face. Mercifully, all she felt was numbness as her vision gradually faded away.

"It's okay, sweetheart. Everything is going to be okay." With a feeble murmur, she spoke her last words before succumbing to the enveloping darkness.

As Harry's body lay on the ocean floor, the mask slowly peeled away from his face, revealing a hollow void where his flesh once was. The meagre amount of energy it had drawn from Harry fuelled a burning desire for more, but it would wait. Its patience was as vast as its hunger. When the moment came, it would manipulate its next host's desires, bend their ambitions toward domination, and drain them with every whispered promise. It had done so before—countless times, across centuries— and each time it fed, it carved another chapter into its long, parasitic legacy. The cycle would begin again. It was only a matter of when.

Ashes of Christmas Past

Ash leaned back on his plush leather recliner with a sigh, settling back into its familiar worn grooves and letting his hands run over the tired and weathered lines in the material. Before him, his son, Blake, played quietly before the electric fireplace set into the bunker wall. Its faux logs lay still, but the flames danced with a quiet intensity.

Blake wore an expression of pure joy as he focused on the toy train set in front of him, pushing and pulling levers and watching in fascination as the train changed tracks, ran through tunnels and over mountains accordingly.

The flickering LED lights of the fireplace were the only source of illumination, casting a warm glow and creating intricate patterns on the walls. The flames replicated those of realities past, swaying gently as if whispering secrets to the night, secrets long since gone from the world it had been created from. Ash let his imagination carry him away from the troubled reality of the present into the past, when the flames danced before people who sat before them, carefree and drinking in merriment. When couples tucked away under blankets on a cozy winter's night before a blazing fire. When people sat before a campfire and told tall tales of horror to scare each other as they drank and enjoyed each other's company. All of that was now lost.

The faint tinny sounds of flames came from the busted speakers below the unit, once holding the ability to mimic the soft crackle of real fire. Despite the obvious artificiality, it was a comforting sound, one that spoke of safety and familiarity, feelings that were now scarce. Ash leaned closer, feeling the warmth on his skin, taking a sip of his eggnog, replicated from the barely operational machine in the kitchen. The flames were not real, but their magic was undeniable, and on this, possibly the last Christmas night his family would ever experience, it was much needed.

The year was 2342. It was the night before Christmas, but unlike anything mentioned in those once much-loved Christmas stories of centuries past, the noise in this warren of bunkers nested together deep underground was far from silent and there were far more dangerous things stirring than a mouse which no longer existed.

The deafening roar of the approaching horde of monsters from above resonated through the underground, reminding those who were fortunate enough to be remaining below the surface of their imminent danger.

Fifty years ago, on Christmas Eve, was the beginning of the end of life as we know it. The Christmas Eve of 2292 had started off like any other. Tired and worn from a day of work, parents diligently prepared houses for their relatives and their rambunctious children, anticipating the chaos of the next day. Their children, brimming with excitement, stayed up past their bedtime, eagerly anticipating Santa's arrival and the delivery of their presents. The parents enjoyed an excessive amount of eggnog while they impatiently waited for the children to fall asleep, allowing them to place the presents under the replicated Christmas tree that emitted a nostalgic, earthy and woody fragrance reminiscent of the actual trees they mimicked.

Meanwhile, a war that had been raging on for centuries was about to come to a bloody and devastating end. Ever since Santa had become part of the Christmas celebrations, humans had poured belief, imagination, and love into the Christmas season in a unified front. As a result, what was once a fictional, mythical character became reality. However, the Santa that was conjured wasn't the traditional present-delivering figure, but rather the guardian of the Christmas spirit. Santa had become the unseen force that filled the Christmas season with a joyous and magical atmosphere. By offering a refuge for connection, he enabled humanity to create and preserve joyful memories that would be passed down through generations. In return, the belief and energy in the season were fed back to the spirit of Santa, ensuring his perpetuity for future generations.

But as with all things, humans had a way of creating the bad along with the good. While Santa had always stolen the spotlight, whispers of Christmas demons lingered in the background. Parents warned their children about Krampus, the beast said to devour and carry away the disobedient kids. There were stories about Belsnickel, who would bring treats to children and then whip them, regardless of their behavior. Then there were stories of the Grinch, the embodiment of anti-Christmas spirit, who would stop at nothing to steal presents and decorations on his mission to ruin Christmas.

Each whisper, story, and tale told empowered the entities, causing them to manifest into reality. Every one of them had banded together to bring a gruesome end to the jolly old red man and his kingdom. Soon after that, they had discovered a means to transcend their own reality and infiltrate ours on Christmas Eve, wreaking havoc and leaving destruction in their wake. Nothing could stop them. Such pure evil energy infused the fiends that even the most well-armed and trained armies were helpless against them. No warhead, whether nuclear or any other type, had the power to harm them; instead, these weapons only added to the destruction of the human race and rendered the land uninhabitable. In a matter of months, humanity was forced to seek shelter underground. The surface became a haunting playground for the monsters and the dwindling number of robot servants, tirelessly scouring the land for nourishment and necessities for those in hiding.

Fifty years and nothing had changed. The demons of Christmas roamed above while the population below slowly dwindled away. Any food that had remained on the surface after the invasion had long since been scavenged. The replicators that were found and retrieved slowly succumbed to age and wear and tear. Some colonies were fortunate to have enough spare parts to repair them and people with the knowledge to do so. Those were the ones that remained today, but the parts supply was almost exhausted, and people who knew how to repair anything technological were now few and far between.

The beasts knew where the humans had fled. They knew the location of every colony, but they left them untouched. Untouched except for that one fateful day each year when they selected one to obliterate. Only five remained now. Five in the entire world. Less than a thousand people in total. In five short years, humans would cease to exist.

A hand landed gently on Ash's shoulder, snapping him out of his thoughts. Looking up, he saw Julie, his wife, gazing down at him with a tender smile. Ash mirrored her smile, his hand finding its way to hers as they both redirected their focus to Blake.

Noticing their attention, Blake looked up at them with a wide, radiant smile on his face.

"Mommy, did you see what I did? I can make the

train go right up this big hill here with just one push of a button," he pointed excitedly at the hill and the button.

"See? Watch." With looks of pure love and adoration on their faces, Julie and Ash watched their son revel in what could be their last Christmas as a family.

At only five years old, Blake was oblivious to the significance of this night. From the moment they found out about Julie's unexpected and unplanned pregnancy, Ash and Julie made a conscious decision to shield their unborn child from the truth of the world. They were determined to preserve his innocence for as long as possible; striving to maintain a sense of normalcy in his life. Part of it was selfishness. They wanted to experience life as a happy family, filled with laughter and love. A bigger part was they wanted to keep Blake happy and carefree as long as they could. In reality, they knew he would likely never reach adulthood.

It wouldn't be long now until the demons above chose their next colony. Throughout the world, armies of the fiends gathered near each remaining one, awaiting the command of their demonic overlords to invade and destroy the weak souls cowering below.

The bunker shook violently, causing rust and dust particles to rain down from the ceiling. Despite being hundreds of feet below the surface, they could still hear the faint noise of belligerent and chaotic cheering from the demonic festivities above.

Blake looked up toward the ceiling, distracted momentarily by the sound, only to return his attention to the toy train set to find the train derailed at the base of the small mountain. Tears filled his eyes, and he stared down at the tracks in despair, as if the incident were the most devastating thing imaginable.

"Oh no! My train! Momma, the shaking ruined everything, make it stop!" he cried as he ran towards Julie with his arms extended, sobs wracking his small body.

Julie enveloped him in her arms, pouring all her love and care into the gesture, as if it had the power to guard him against anything the world might throw his way.

"It's okay sweetie, it will be over soon," she whispered to him, rocking him gently.

Blake nestled into Julie's arms, sniffling softly as the cacophony from above intensified. The tinsel in the room swayed above them while the jingle of the tree's decorations created a curious contrast against the noise on the surface. A decision was imminent, and soon Ash, Julie and the blissfully unaware Blake would know their fate.

In a land where magic reigned, a place that our imaginations created and where the Christmas spirit thrived, a lone and battered factory stood amongst the ashes of the once vibrant and pristine landscape. The banging and ringing of hammers on steel could be heard for miles, though the only living beings inhabiting the land left were those causing the hammering.

Inside, a dozen diminutive elves worked diligently and with desperation, putting the finishing touches on a machine that they hoped would bring about salvation for all once more.

The once pristine, green and yellow uniforms of the emaciated elves now hung off their frail bodies, stained with soot and tattered from endless days and nights of work following the massacre of Santa and most of his workers by the demonic beings of Christmas.

Of the workforce of once over two hundred elves, these were the last survivors. Thirty had survived the initial massacre, but over time, more had succumbed to crippling grief, and starvation. Others buckled under the weight of depression, deciding to end their lives rather than struggle in a life they no longer held hope for. Despite the growing scarcity of food and water, and the desperation that accompanied it, the elves had continued to work tirelessly. Now they were on the brink of finishing what they hoped would be the end of all their problems. A machine capable of reconstructing Santa, including all of his memories. A machine that held all the hopes and dreams of all those in the past. One that fed on the remaining magic that had steadily faded from the world of humanity.

Alfie set his hammer aside, his tired hands trembling as he looked up with anticipation at the machine. He, like his fellow elves, had put everything into this contraption. All that remained was the simple act of pushing a button. One button press that would either bring about salvation or despair.

"Well, I guess this is it then," Wren weakly uttered beside him, leaning on him for support.

"Yeah, this is it," Alfie said, his arms encircling her in a warm and comforting hug.

As if that act alone were a signal, the remaining elves formed a circle, their hands intertwined.

Humming together as one, they swayed back and forth, lost in the tune, creating their own magic together one last time.

Ash stood in the bedroom, performing a final inspection of the shotgun and ammunition he had laid out on the bed. The sudden sound of blaring alarms shattered the silence, signalling the decision. Their community had been chosen.

His chest tightened, and his heart sank as the realization hit him. This was it. He was going to lose everything. But it wouldn't come without a cost, he vowed. He had one weapon that others in the community did not. A sentry bot he had been working on for years. Of the five scavenger bots he used to have, one of them had found and brought back the battered remains of a sentry bot. Though it was half-destroyed, Ash had the technical knowledge to repair it. He had just needed the parts. Over time, he gained them through trade, bartering items his bot had discovered, which held no interest to him, in exchange for the parts he required.

He had put the final touches to the unit only a few

months ago, but it worked. The bot had sprung to life and had functioned exactly as it should have. He'd even been able to make some improvements to its initial design. Featuring a range of defensive and offensive capabilities, the bot was a master of both long and short-range combat. Ash had even programmed it with the addition of various martial art modules he had custom-built. The bot would be a capable killing machine, one that he hoped might just be enough to save him and his family.

With a commanding gesture, Krampus guided his deranged troupe of Christmas demons and enslaved elves into the yawning mouth of the hatch he had torn open.

There would be no stopping them now. In his mind, he could already envision the massacre taking place below, and the agonized screams of the first victims were like sweet music to him.

As the flow of twisted Christmas monsters continued to pour down the hatch, a smile spread across his face from ear to ear. Possessed reindeers, horns decorated with dried entrails, their red eyes glowing with hate, leapt down the shaft. Elves in advanced stages of decay, their skeletons partially exposed, struggled to maintain their balance on their reanimated limbs. Some fell into the abyss below, while others clumsily descended the ladder, their insane laughter echoing as the corrupt spirits within them delighted in their every motion. Filled with chaos, the Yule cat released a piercing shriek that mimicked a meow, its radiant eyes fixed on the shaft as it advanced. Every movement it made spoke of evil intent. A horde of wild-looking Straggele, demonic beings from ancient folklore, jostled and brawled as they made their way to the shaft. Covered in thick, matted fur, their bodies were twisted and grotesque. Long, curved horns jutted from their heads, and their faces were a nightmarish blend of human and beast, with eyes lit up with an unnatural glow. They cackled with anticipation, already imagining the havoc they would wreak on the unsuspecting victims below.

Krampus chuckled. Soon it would be his turn, then the party would really start.

This was it. Ash had done all that he could to prepare for this moment. Each corridor leading to their bunker had two sentry guns stationed outside the entrance, creating a formidable line of defense. Each entrance was blocked by closed and welded heavy steel doors. They would hold for a while, but Ash held no illusions that they would fall. The sentry bot was activated and stationed at the entrance to the master bedroom, its shining metallic appearance offering a ray of hope despite the over-whelming challenge ahead.

Ash and his family were fortunate to have their home on the bottom level of the colony. The bottom level was reserved for those who had children and was the safest area to be. Their colony had upped its defenses each time one of the remaining few had been overcome, taking the lessons learned from their downfall and applying them to their own colony in hopes it might withstand an attack when it inevitably came. Thus far, no defense had been successful, but there was always a chance that one might be someday. Ash hoped more than anything that today would be that day.

Fear gripped Ash and Julie as they huddled in the master bedroom, their hearts pounding in response to the faint sounds of explosives and sentry guns in the distance.

Julie had Blake on her lap, doing her best to keep him entertained and distracted. Blake was busy playing with a partially burnt and incomplete building block set that had been salvaged many years ago. With a pair of sound-proof headphones on, he was in a state of blissful igno-rance, oblivious to the pandemonium unfolding outside.

Ash and Julie locked eyes, exchanging concerned looks that spoke volumes. She was doing her best to be the calm and attentive mother, but Ash could see the slight trembling of her body as fear took hold. Ash reached over, placing his hand on top of hers and gave it a reassuring squeeze. He longed to comfort her, to assure her that everything would be alright, but deep down, he knew that their world would never be the same, no matter what lay ahead.

Outside, the explosions and gunfire began to die down, replaced by screams of terror and agonizing pain. It was time.

Ash stood up, his legs quivering with fear. The

colony's defenses had clearly faltered, taking much less time to collapse than he had expected. The forces outside must be fearsome indeed. Even though the sentry guns at the perimeter of their hovel remained inactive, he knew it was time to take his position in the lounge room and lock and secure the master bedroom doors behind him.

Ash made his way over to Julie and Blake, his heart heavy with the impending goodbyes. Blake felt the encroaching presence of his father's shadow as he clicked another brick into place, his face lighting up with a bright smile as he looked up at him. Ash's heart melted in an instant. Knowing that it might be his last chance, he studied every feature on Blake's face, capturing every minuscule detail. If he was going to die, he was going to do it with his family pictured at the forefront of his mind.

Sliding the headphones off Blake's ears, Ash said softly, "Hey buddy. Having fun?"

Blake nodded happily. "Look, Daddy, I've almost finished. It's us, see?"

He pointed to the scene he had been building. It was a replica of the bunker they were in, complete with a Christmas tree and a fireplace and three figures sitting down at a table, tiny plates of food set before them.

"See?" he said, pointing at each figure in turn. "That's me, you, and Mommy."

"Wait... Who's that?" Ash said, spotting another figure outside the entrance of the bunker.

"Oh, that's Santa. He's waiting for me to go to bed so he can deliver my presents."

"Oh, I see," Ash said, nodding.

"It looks fantastic, buddy. We'd better make sure you get to bed early tonight then so that Santa can come in time."

Blake's face lit up with excitement, his wide grin accompanied by an enthusiastic nod.

"But before that, Daddy just has to do a few chores. Can you be a big brave boy and protect Mommy while I'm gone?"

Blake nodded solemnly, his excited expression now replaced by a determined one.

"Don't worry, Daddy, I'll look after Mommy," he said, his sincere tone tugging at Ash's heartstrings.

"Good boy, now put these back on for a while and keep playing. I'll just talk to Mommy for a bit, okay?"

Blake nodded and refocused on the building block set, his attention drawn back to the small pile of bricks he had remaining.

Julie and Ash walked to the door together. Without a word, she wrapped her arms around him, holding on tightly as if every ounce of her being depended on it, aware that this could be their last embrace.

He pulled back just enough to gaze into her eyes, planting a tender kiss on her lips. Pulling her head to his chest, he softly ran his fingers through her hair, feeling the warmth of her tears through his shirt.

"I love you, baby," he whispered into her ear. "I'm so thankful for you and Blake. You've made me the happiest guy alive, you know that?"

Holding him tighter, she sobbed, her body racked with emotion.

As they separated a few minutes later, Julie discreetly brushed away the remaining tears, not wanting to upset Blake.

"When I close this door, you need to seal it with the blowtorch. If everything goes well, I'll knock or call out for you to unseal it once it's all over."

Julie gave a silent nod, too afraid to say anything in case she started crying once more.

Ash grabbed the shotgun and satchel of bullets and headed towards the door, stealing one last glance at Blake and Julie before he departed. He heard her whispering one final, "I love you," as he shut the door behind him. As he leaned against it, he could feel the weight of his emotions crashing over him, tears streaming down his face as he let himself go. This would be the last time he would allow himself to shed tears. From here, he would need to steel himself and prepare for the impending chaos.

After collecting himself and hearing the welding begin on the bedroom door behind him, Ash walked towards the overturned sofa, positioned in front of the doors where the horrifying sounds were coming from. He sat with his back against it, closing his eyes and concentrating on slowing down his breath.

The sudden noise of the sentry guns coming to life outside the door jolted him back into focus. They were coming. The hallway filled with the cacophony of enraged screeches and pained cries as the sentry guns mercilessly rained bullets upon the fiends. They had encountered resistance on the way here, but it was nothing like this. The deafening sounds outside grew louder as the strategically placed claymores on the approach to their bunker were triggered, their explosions reverberating through the air. As if on cue, the sentry guns stopped their relentless firing, creating an eerie silence. The beasts outside had seemingly retreated for now, no doubt regrouping from the unexpected force of the resistance. With a wary eye, Ash directed his focus to the entrance across from him. He expected the next attack to come from there as the monstrosities outside searched for any weaknesses they could exploit.

As expected, it didn't take long for the sentry guns on that side to come alive, their mechanical roaring filling the air. The explosions from the claymores echoed through the bunker, their thunderous booms causing the LED lights above to flicker, casting erratic shadows on the walls as the entire bunker trembled.

The sound of gunfire ceased a few moments later, and Ash let out a slow breath, savoring the sudden stillness. It couldn't be possible that he had actually managed to repel the demonic things, could it? He couldn't let himself believe it, but the silence replacing the sound of destruction was deafening.

Minutes passed with no further sounds from either corridor, and Ash found himself daring to believe it was over. Just as he was about to stand up and head back towards the bedroom doors to ask Julie to unseal them, the deafening sounds of gunfire erupted once again, this time coming from both sides simultaneously. Suddenly, he heard the deep, reverberating bellows of an enormous beast approaching, causing Ash to crouch back behind the sofa. His hands wrapped around his shotgun in a tight grip, his heart pounding.

Upon hearing the screeching of metal in the corridor and the sudden ceasing of gunfire, Ash's hope crumbled like a fragile glass. The room trembled as the massive figure behind the sealed bunker door crashed into it, causing Christmas decorations to fall, and dishes to fly and shatter upon hitting the ground.

The door couldn't hold for much longer. Howls of fury filled the air as the beast relentlessly attacked the door, its assault causing cracks to appear in the once secure welding. Ash placed his shotgun on the upturned sofa, aligning it towards the door. With one final powerful blow, the door burst open, scattering shards of metal in every direction. Smoke billowed through the entrance, carrying with it the unmistakable scent of death and the sharp tang of shrapnel. Ash strained to discern any signs of movement.

The smoke swirled within the confines of the room, its tendrils exploring in all directions as if in search of a way out. Through the haze, a gigantic shape materialized. The monster, hunched and contorted, stood at almost the same height as the bunker, its appearance a horrifying fusion of human and animal. The smoke could not hide the piercing glow of its amber eyes, which reflected the malevolence within. Its grin widened, and as it locked eyes with Ash, the glint of sharpened teeth became unmistakable. As it approached, the details of its appearance became clear.

Jutting from its angular skull were horns, curved and serrated, with each tip honed to a lethal sharpness. Its form, hooded as it was, conveyed its otherworldly origins. Its skin clung to its bones, appearing parchment thin and etched with runes of suffering. The clomp of its footsteps as it approached revealed its cloven hooves, black as midnight, as its breath soured the smoke-filled air.

Studying Ash intently, the demon cocked its head to the side, its forked tongue sampling the air. The stench of fear coming from Ash and his family, locked away in the bedroom behind him, was like a feast to the fiend's senses.

This was Krampus, a nightmare and myth come to life.

Ignoring the weakness overtaking his body, Ash's trembling finger reached for the trigger of the shotgun as he stared in disbelief at the monstrosity before him.

The deafening sound of the gun blast echoed through the bunker, accompanied by a brilliant flash that sent the abomination reeling backwards, disappearing into the thick smoke. Ash had hit it; he was sure of it. The beast's furious bellow reverberated through the air, signalling its imminent attack as it charged through the swirling smoke, hurtling toward Ash. Despite the impending collision, Ash somehow found the composure to fire off one last shot before the demon collided with him and the sofa. It was no use; the shotgun had done nothing. The runes on the beast's leathery skin were aglow, protecting it from any damage the gun may have done.

The creature loomed over Ash, its towering figure casting a dark shadow as its enormous, clawed hand closed in on him. As the monstrosity snarled at him, its fingertips found and slowly penetrated Ash's chest, causing excruciating pain. All he could see was the other-worldly amber glow of its eyes, which seemed to hold an endless depth. Approaching the bedroom door, the demon raised him into the air, Ash's screams echoing through the room. Helpless, Ash could only squirm and weep while the beast exerted its strength, pushing against the door with its other hand. The metal groaned and protested, but eventually succumbed, revealing his wife and son huddled together against the wall, their faces etched with terror.

"N...No..." With a scream of desperation, Ash pounded his hands down on Krampus's arm. Swinging its head around, it locked eyes with him before turning its attention back to Julie and Blake. Its teeth glistened as it grinned at them.

Just then, the sentry bot leapt into action. As soon as it detected Ash in the demon's grasp, it immediately processed the situation and concluded that the only course of action available to it was to engage in short-distance combat. Its movements were calculated and precise as it attacked the beast, aiming to incapacitate with every punch and kick. Krampus glanced down at the machine, a smile playing on its lips as the runes on its body ignited, nullifying the bot's futile attacks. In a single, devastating swipe of its hand, the bot was rendered useless, its once sleek exterior now reduced to a heap of twisted scrap metal. Ash could only let out a feeble moan, his lips stained with blood, his head drooping as he fought to stay conscious.

With an eerie calmness, Krampus hoisted Ash's squirming form, presenting him in a macabre fashion to his family. Its other hand reached out, touching Ash's chest before ruthlessly puncturing it with its razor-like fingertips. Blood sprayed from Ash's mouth, filling it to overflowing as it splattered onto the floor. His eyes widened in shock, unable to tear his sight away from the vision of his crying family. With a terrifying snarl, the monster plunged its fingers deeper into his chest and pulled them apart, shattering his bones and causing a horrifying explosion of flesh and gore that splattered the walls. The screams of Julie and Blake filled the bunker with anguish. Julie clasped Blake to her chest, doing everything she could to shield him from the gruesome sight that surrounded them.

With a sinister grin, Krampus locked eyes with her and pried her arms away from Blake, its bony fingers digging into her skin as it clasped her in its grasp. The beast lifted her towards its face. Her desperate cries for Blake cut through the air as the pungent stench of its breath invaded her senses. In her last moments, she mustered the strength to say, "I love you," to her terrified son before the tightening grip of Krampus silenced her with a sickening snap of bones, her body falling limp in its grasp. Letting her body fall to the floor, Krampus approached and reached down toward the desperate and scrambling boy as he tried to crawl under the bed.

Krampus's claw barely had a chance to secure its hold on Blake's legs before it slackened. In a macabre display, Krampus's chest erupted in a shower of bone and viscera, drenching the already stained walls. Confusion flickered briefly in its eyes before the glow within was forever extinguished, as the monstrosity collapsed to the floor.

Blake looked up in terror, expecting something else just as horrifying to take its place, but instead a feeling of peace and love enveloped him, instantly stifling any feelings of shock and trauma.

The presence enveloping the room spoke of kindness, of joy, of love, of everything his family had given him in its purest form, and it was emanating from a figure behind the now stilled body of Krampus.

Blake looked in wonder at the figure approaching him, its wrinkled, kind eyes promising assurances of peace and a future free of worries. Its jolly presence, the familiar red floppy hat and uniform and bone-white beard, spoke of only one possibility. Santa had returned.

Behind him, the tiny forms of elves, dressed in vivid green uniforms, meticulously cleared the room of debris and gore, leaving no trace behind.

Their job done, Wren and Alfie's eyes, filled with Elven grace, met each other's with pride before they shifted their focus back to Santa, who had Blake wrapped up in a comforting embrace.

A few minutes later, Santa rose, holding Blake's hand, and walked over to Wren and Alfie. With a knowing smile, he placed Blake's hand into Wren's, while Alfie took the other. Together, they made their way back to the hatch and up to the surface, where Santa's sleigh awaited. Santa's kingdom lay ahead, and with it, the hope that Blake could once again be reunited with his parents through the reconstruction machine, all thanks to the efforts of the elves, led by Wren and Alfie.

The Moon's Kiss

"I think that's the last of them," Joe said wearily as he ejected the empty shell from his Mossberg 500 shotgun.

"It better be," Mack said, as he slid down the cave wall to the ground in exhaustion. "We're running on fumes here. I'm not sure about you, but I'm just about out of ammunition too."

Joe nodded in agreement; a check of his backpack confirmed his stock was perilously low too.

"Let's rest here for a short while. We've still got a long way to go, and we should use the daylight while we have it."

Pulling out his map, Joe marked their position, his finger tracing a path to their next destination, a town called Langmire.

"Three klicks," he muttered to himself, checking his watch. "We should be able to make it."

With a sigh of exhaustion, he plopped down beside

Mack and began searching through his pack. He retrieved two high-energy snack bars from his rations kit, offering one to Mack.

Joe reflected on the task before them as he chewed, battling the feeling of hopelessness and not for the first time.

Six months ago, a near-extinction-level event had devastated the world. Giant unstoppable meteors, the remains of the moon, had rained down with incredible force onto every continent of the planet. The cause of the moon's implosion remains unknown to this day. Scientists had rushed to find a solution to the approaching rock storm and the devastation that was to come. They had found none. Last-ditch missile launches had neutralized the smaller meteors, but the massive ones proved to be the ultimate harbingers of destruction, eradicating 80% of the population in a single day.

As the remaining leaders scrambled to organize order amidst the chaos, an additional threat rose. From deep within the earth, something awoke. An organism that had lain dormant for centuries had stirred, disturbed by the destruction on the surface and the resulting vibrations felt down to the earth's core.

It wasted no time in sending a horde of its children, gigantic insectoid-like creatures, to the surface and laid waste to the remaining population.

It was only through the heroics of a single army commander, Jethro, that anyone had survived at all. Performing a training drill in a military compound in the Chihuahuan desert at the time of the attack, he had fearlessly organized their defenses, destroying any monster that came their way. Since they were so far away from the primary hubs of civilization, they hadn't encountered as much force, enabling them to take stock of the enemy and do some basic research.

Scouting missions were undertaken, which increasingly turned into rescue missions as they found survivors, the base turning into a mini city after a few months.

The team led by the commander developed a makeshift atomic bomb after finding enough materials during salvage operations. The aim was to destroy the nest of insects they had located and put a stop to the infestation once and for all.

Joe and Mack were part of the last salvage operation. They were on a mission to recover a uranium bullet from an underground warehouse near Alarmagordo, the final component needed for the bomb. It had not gone smoothly. A group of beasts had ambushed their squad as they left to begin their journey back to the base after retrieving the bullet. Joe and Mack were the only two to survive out of the dozen sent on the mission.

Joe rose to his feet and kicked the dead insectoid thing lying just outside the cave's entrance, channelling all his pent-up anger and frustration into it. The insectoid thing lay curled up, reminding Joe of the way spiders curled into themselves on death. Its ice-cold blue bulbous eyes set into a crystalline skull stared vacantly at him. Even in death, he could see the cunning intelligence that had made these beasts so dangerous. A hardened, ashen gray colored exoskeleton bare of skin formed its body.

Hardened sacks made of a harsh, leathery material protected its innards underneath the exoskeleton. Attached to its spine was a whip-like tail lined with razor-sharp barbs. Long skewer-like fingers were attached to each of its four double-jointed limbs, which it used to propel itself along the surface at incredible speed and tunnel into the earth below.

Green liquid had pooled underneath the abomination, its lifeblood oozing from the buckshot Joe had emptied into it. Its body was the only weakness, the head remaining impervious to every weapon they had tried so far.

"Alright, Mack, time to get moving while we still have light."

With a groan, Mack rose to his feet, his muscles seizing up after a long day of combat. The temporary respite had only served to remind him how fatigued his body was. "How far to the next checkpoint?"

"Three klicks. We should be able to make it by nightfall if we hustle."

Performing a once-over on his weapon, he slung his backpack over his shoulders and said, "Let's get a move on then."

The pair exited the cave and set a fast pace. Their next stop would be their last before they reached the base. After spending a week out on this mission, they were both eager to have a shower and get a hot meal in their bellies.

The journey passed uneventfully, with only a few sightings of the giant insects in the distance, but the pair managed to stay out of sight. By the time they reached Langmire, there was still enough daylight to find an empty house to shelter in. Spotting a suitable one, they entered to find dried bloodstains on the walls, but no signs of any further recent activity, so they settled in for the night. There were three rooms with beds still made. Joe and Mack took one each before meeting in the kitchen to discuss the plan for the coming day.

There were still twenty klicks to travel to get back to base, which meant they should arrive at around noon the following day if they left early enough. The route was a dangerous one. There were no additional towns or buildings along the route from Langmire to the base. Only the harsh rock and sand-filled terrain stood between them and salvation. Routine clearing operations had dampened the number of insectoids that occupied that space, but they had no way of knowing when the last sweep was completed so it was likely they would encounter more of them along the way.

Next, they took stock of the weapons and ammunition they had remaining, laying them out on the table. Six grenades, eighty rifle rounds, and thirty shotgun shells remained in their meagre supply. The pair exchanged worried glances, their brows furrowed in concern. It would be enough if they didn't encounter many of the monsters on their way, but if they encountered a group, it would likely mean the end of them.

After cleaning their weapons and repacking their ammunition, they retired to their rooms. Anxiety filled both of them about the journey ahead, but they had become accustomed to sleeping under the constant threat of danger. As such, they went to bed with hope for a restful night.

It wasn't to be. Joe woke up in the pitch-black room to the terror-filled, high-pitched screams of his comrade as the sound of a violent struggle drifted down the hallway.

Grabbing the shotgun leaning against the wall by his bed, he ran to Mack's room, fearing the worst.

A sickening crunch followed by a choked gurgle greeted him as he arrived outside the door, taking position there and peering in at the scene.

Mack was lying on a blood-soaked bed, pinned down by one of the giant insects with needle-like fingers piercing through his chest into the mattress. Another limb had him by his throat, and Joe watched on, frozen in horror, as it snapped his neck and left it barely attached to his body as a torrent of blood gushed out.

The thing let out a chittering sound as it turned and noticed Joe frozen in the doorway, retracting its fingers from Mack's chest as it prepared to launch itself at him.

"You son of a bitch!" Joe let out a powerful roar, feeling a surge of adrenaline as his training instincts took over. Aiming his shotgun, he squeezed the trigger, the loud boom of the gunshot echoing in his ears as his first shot soared high, narrowly grazing the top of the insect's crystalline skull. It was enough to snap its head backward, the force of the blow sending the thing stumbling before it regained its balance, fury clear in its alien eyes.

Not giving it a chance to recover, Joe ejected the

spent shell and blasted it again, this one peppering the right limb and blowing off a few of the beast's needle-sharp fingers and sending it crashing into the nearby wall.

Taking the opportunity to reload, Joe advanced into the room as the insect lurched away from the wall, screeching at Joe as it leaped into the air toward him, claws outstretched.

Joe planted his feet and aimed directly at the center mass of its body as it flew towards him, blasting a round into its abdomen. The resulting explosion sent bone and doughy flesh throughout the room as it crashed to the floor beside him in a heap.

"Mack!" Joe cried as he dropped the shotgun to the floor and ran to the bed, sinking down beside it in grief.

Mack and Joe had come up through the army ranks together. The first day they had met as fresh recruits had immediately cemented a friendship that had lasted through the years. With Mack gone, he was now truly alone, having lost his parents and siblings in the initial meteor strikes. The reality of the situation struck him like a thunderbolt, his eyes welling up with tears as a wave of loss and grief washed over him. Eventually, his eyelids grew heavy with exhaustion, and he slipped into uncon-sciousness.

Joe woke up on the floor to a stream of sunlight shining into his eyes through the window across from him. Rubbing his tired eyes, he mustered his strength and slung his backpack over his shoulder, making sure his shotgun was loaded for the journey ahead.

Placing a hand on Mack's arm, he hung his head and uttered a prayer. His final whispered "Goodbye" sent tears trickling down his cheeks once more.

Taking a deep breath to compose himself, Joe left the town and his friend behind. He was close to the end of his journey now, and he was focused more than ever on ending these abomination's reign of devastation once and for all.

Signs of destruction and insect activity were all around him and increased as he neared the base. Mortar impact craters, along with bullet holes, had carved notches into the surface of the dry desert. On the ground, the still-recent splashes of greenish alien blood stood out against the dark orange of the environment around him. The number of scattered alien body parts and carcasses increased as he pressed forward, his pace slowed by having to find paths through the carnage. Finally, as he reached the base of a hill, the compound slowly came into view, the sight of it filling him with relief. It wouldn't be long now before he could avenge Mack and put an end to these bastards once and for all. Filled with anticipation, he crested the hill and immediately stopped in his tracks, stunned at the sight before him.

The mile-high wall made of concrete and steel that once kept the base safe was now in ruins, with beasts swarming around in a hive of activity. Crouching low behind a nearby boulder, he pulled out his binoculars and zoomed in on the group, only to drop them in horror and take a step back, his face turning pale.

The insects were carrying and piling bodies in a heap just outside the wall. Body parts, scattered flesh, and organs were strewn haphazardly as the bodies were thrown carelessly toward the heap, most of them having been torn apart in clear fury. Some carried people who were still wriggling weakly before their resistance was put to an end as the insect's talons carved through their flesh.

Joe heaved the meagre contents of his stomach onto the ground beside him as panic set in. This was the only known bastion of humanity left, and it was gone, along with the weapon that could have been their salvation, the last piece of which he held in his possession.

Panicked breaths racked his body as images of people he had known in the base flashed before his eyes. Those who he had fought beside, his squad mates, whom he had trained with for years, the staff, many of whom had become his friends—all were gone. The burden of his past trauma, the overwhelming feeling of hopelessness, the losses he had suffered and the impending death that loomed over him became unbearable, pushing his already strained mind to the brink. Anxiety overtook him, and he surrendered to the comforting embrace of enveloping darkness.

Opening his eyes to the darkness of night, Joe lay still, letting himself gradually adjust to wakefulness. His muscles, held taut with anxiety, ached as if he'd been through twelve rounds in a losing bout in a boxing ring. The sharp pang of pins and needles replaced the ache as he deliberately massaged each limb in turn to get the blood flow moving once again.

With his heart still pounding, he sat up straight and took a few deep breaths, performing a brief meditation to regain his composure before rising to his feet stiffly. Picking up the binoculars he had abandoned in panic earlier, he once again focused on the remains of the base. The pile of bodies had grown, the movement of the insects had lost the frantic energy of before, doubtless running out of the supply to grow the stack further.

Shifting his focus, he surveyed the rest of the base and found to his surprise that despite the damage to the wall, the rest of the buildings seemed relatively intact. Locating the building housing the atomic weapon, he saw it had largely been untouched. Maybe the insects had an instinctual awareness of the hidden peril it held for them.

Joe gathered and readied his weapons, clipping the remaining grenades to his belt for easy access, and looped the belt of shotgun shells around his shoulder.

Taking one last deep breath, he steeled himself and used the cover of darkness to dash toward the area of the wall where the concentration of monsters was thinnest. He reached it and held his breath, straining to hear any sign of movement that would indicate he had been discovered, but exhaled in relief when it remained silent. Peering around the wall, saw only a few of the insects milling about near the body pile. Sickening crunches from their direction suggested they were otherwise occupied.

Setting himself for the last run, he unclipped two of the grenades, pulled the pin off one, and hurled it toward the tower of bodies. As the explosion erupted with immense force, viscera and chunks of flesh soared through the air and clouded it with a mist of blood. Taking advantage of the opportunity, he sprinted toward the bomb facility.

The insects let out furious, inhuman screeches from behind as they gave chase, swiftly gaining ground on him. Without hesitation, Joe yanked the pin off the second grenade and launched it into the midst of the pursuing beings, the explosion scattering them in all directions and buying him some extra time.

Reaching the building, he flung the door open, leaning his back against it only long enough to regain his breath before piling any furniture he could find against it. It wouldn't last for long, but hopefully, it would last long enough for what he needed to do. With that done, he made his way to the securely locked area at the back of the building, where the brightly flashing red key card scanner next to the heavyset metal door awaited him.

In a state of nervousness, he fumbled for his card, his hands shaking. Casting an anxious glance over his shoulder towards the entrance, he breathed a sigh of relief as the door finally opened. He rushed through, ensuring he closed it firmly behind him. He sighed in relief at the sight of the rocket housing the bomb, which had already been pre-programmed to target the insect's nest, still sitting safely and securely in place below the half-open roof above. Seeing that the roof was already partially open prompted him to examine it more closely. The roof should only have opened once the launch sequence had begun. It was then that he noticed the deep indentations and scratches that he had missed during his initial cursory glance.

"Shit," he cursed under his breath, his jaw tightening. The faint sound of legs skittering toward him from the shadowy corner of the facility made him curse again, his grip on the shotgun tightening as he prepared for what was coming. Using it with the bomb so close was reckless —but if he wanted to live long enough to insert the cylinder and finish the device, he might not have a choice.

An insect came into view, letting out a piercing screech as it leaped toward him. Joe steadied his aim and fired. The deafening blast made his ears ring as it tore through its exoskeleton and spilled its insides to the ground, sending it collapsing to the floor in a lifeless heap.

The door behind him flew open with a crash, the pile of furniture used as a barricade, unable to withstand the onslaught of the creatures as they poured through.

"No!" Joe screamed as he grabbed the cylinder case from his pack and hastened towards the control panel at the base of the rocket. He punched the key to slide open the cylinder compartment, but felt his back being torn open as an insect viciously sliced into his flesh from behind. He fought through the pain, reaching for the compartment with the cylinder in hand—just as another appendage speared into him. The force tore him off his feet, hurled him backward, and slammed his head against the rocket. Stars burst behind his eyes. The cylinder case spilled to the ground and rolled out of his view as he slid down onto the floor, the torn flesh of his back resting against the rocket control panel. Struggling to move, his ruined body could only manage to topple onto its side. Consumed by despair and a deep sense of hopelessness, he could do nothing but emit faint groans, his tears mingling with the blood that spilled from his mouth.

The open roof above him bathed the writhing mass of approaching insects in the glow of dawn. Joe's vision was fading, but he managed to catch a glimpse of the sun as it began to rise, casting a warm glow over the opening. His eyes beheld a dawn that would never be seen by a human again.

Deadly Bytes

Detective Dave Calahan sat back in his chair, wearing a satisfied smile after making the final adjustment to his horrifying animatronic bugbear. After a few moments of rest, he rose to his feet and double-checked his work, ensuring everything was in place before closing the panel on the back of the imposing six-foot monster. Grabbing a USB cable from the bench, he inserted it into the hidden slot beneath the panel, then connected it to the USB port on his computer. Now, all that remained was to test all of its features, and then he could finally call it a night.

Dave, an enthusiastic lover of horror and fantasy, had been designing and constructing animatronic beasts since his early twenties, even before he ventured into a career in law enforcement. Despite having less free time nowadays, he still managed to complete a few of the monstrosities each month. It was an expensive hobby, but he loved it, and there was nothing like bringing a monster from his worst nightmares to life. He even sold some of them to his friends and acquaintances when Halloween rolled around. The bugbear, a terrifying amalgamation of demon and bear, all fur, teeth and claws, would stay with him in his horror room, adding to the collection of terrifying creatures. The werewolf, giant spider, zombie, and demon were already there, each capable of realistic movements and eerie sound effects.

Sitting down at the computer, he tapped a few keys to bring up his simple but effective custom-made control software and tapped on the button to raise the beast's arm. With a mechanical whir, the bugbear's arm extended obediently upwards. He pressed the button to bring it down, and the beast's arm swung down smoothly and rested at its side. He systematically clicked on each button, testing every function of the construct until he was satisfied. With a yawn, he settled into his chair and glanced at his watch, only to be startled by the glowing green clock face, which read 1:12 am.

"Shit," he muttered under his breath, hastily rolling his chair back and springing to his feet. With a 7:30 am wake-up call looming, he knew the exhaustion of starting the work week with little sleep would be hard to shake.

Just as he was heading towards his bedroom, his work phone started buzzing in his pocket. He let out a frustrated sigh. It seemed like he wouldn't get any rest tonight.

Retrieving his phone from his pocket, he accepted the call, already bracing himself for a long night ahead.

The moment he noticed the officer's expression of shock on his pale face at the entrance of the run-down apartment building as he pulled up; he realized what awaited him would be anything but pleasant. The dilapidated building exuded an air of neglect and decay, with peeling paint and broken windows. After nodding to the officer at the door, he stepped into the hallway and was met with an overpowering stench, forcing him to quickly pinch his nose. The floor was a mess, with rubbish scattered everywhere. Rare glimpses of the ground through the rubbish revealed decaying floorboards underneath. The walls were stained yellow and peeling, revealing the layers beneath. The stairs directly in front of him were flanked by a rusting metal guardrail, with several sections missing. In the small space behind the stairs, discarded bags of trash had been left to rot as flies buzzed lazily around them. Dave's face twisted in disgust, feeling his stomach churn and his gorge rise. He could deal with the horror of almost any crime scene, but it turns out that the smell of decaying garbage was his Achilles heel.

Keeping his nose pinched, Dave made his way up to the second floor and down a narrow hallway to apartment 223. Ducking under the police tape, he ran into the photographer Mark, who had just wrapped up and was heading to the door. His face was as pale as the police officer's guarding the entrance downstairs.

"Hey Mark, what have we got?"

"A big damn mess, that's what," Mark said with a grimace. "In all my years of photographing fucked-up crime scenes, this one is pretty high up there." He paused, a visible shudder running down his body. "Now if you'll excuse me, I have to get these processed and then wash my eyes out with bleach. See you at the station later?"

Dave nodded and pressed himself against the wall as Mark, clearly shaken, hurried past him toward the exit, eager to leave.

Dave shrugged and pressed forward, only to come to an abrupt stop as he turned the corner, his eyes widening at the sight of the horrifying scene that greeted him.

The living room stretched out in front of him, a nightmarish scene of carnage. Blood stained every inch, with bits of flesh and body organs clinging to the walls, ceiling, sofa, TV, and its stand. Next to the overturned sofa, the remnants of the victim's body lay in a gruesome heap. Scattered across the room were numerous drones of varying sizes, from palm-sized to over a meter long, some broken while others remained whole, but all with blades stained with blood.

"Looks like the damn drones came to life and attacked the poor bastard."

Sam, the medical examiner, rose to his feet from his position near a numbered tag where a blood-coated drone lay overturned.

"It certainly looks that way," Dave remarked, taking

in the sight of the number tags, the bloody drones, and the deep, jagged cuts on what remained of the body.

"The wounds match the blades perfectly. There are no other marks on the body that would indicate another weapon was used, but an autopsy will confirm that. There are no signs of forced entry. The door was still locked from the inside, and the windows were also all locked from the inside."

"So, either the guy was terrible at controlling his drones, or someone else was controlling them remotely."

"Seems that way," Sam nodded in agreement.

"Wait, what's that?" Dave asked, his attention drawn to a blinking red light on an otherwise dark computer monitor in the corner.

"Don't know, but I'll leave you to it. I'll organize forensics and transport for the body."

Dave waved in response as he stepped around the bloodstains and viscera to get to the workstation. In stark contrast to the rest of the building and the old and warn contents in this apartment, the PC under the desk appeared to be state-of-the art. The monitor on the desk was small but seemed to be similarly high tech.

Now that he was closer to it, he could see the screen was flashing with the same red words appearing at regular intervals on an otherwise black screen.

Connect Phone to USB to unlock

Pulling on some rubber gloves he had stuffed into his pockets, he tapped on the keyboard, hoping that it was just a screensaver, but there was no response.

With his eyebrows furrowed in curiosity, he bent

down to examine the PC below the desk. As he suspected, he found a USB cable plugged into the front slot of the PC, which had fallen onto the floor during the attack. Lifting it up, he saw the flat, rectangular head of a USB-C connector. Standing back up, he scanned the room, his eyes landing on the victim's phone a few meters away. Its screen was shattered, and deep cuts marked the casing, mirroring the injuries on the body.

Sighing in frustration, Dave fished out his work phone from his pocket. Luckily, his department was not stingy in its funding, so he had the latest iPhone, which would fit the cable, but he knew plugging it in would be a bad idea. He should call in the tech guys to handle it. He glanced at his watch: 4:25 am. Jack, his boss, was always on his ass about getting his cases wrapped up faster, and he was already way behind in his paperwork. If he found something now, it might keep him off his back, at least for a day or two. Besides, it wasn't as if it were his personal phone. If something were to happen to his work phone, he could easily get it replaced.

Shrugging, he set his phone on the table and plugged in the cable. In response, the monitor flickered to life, displaying a mesmerizing, multicolored loading icon for a moment before revealing a web browser logged into a website. It only took a few seconds for him to realise this wasn't any regular browser. It was the Tor browser, known for its use in navigating the dark web.

With a few clicks, he uncovered the use of a VPN, a tool that cloaks online activity, adding an extra layer of secrecy. A further glance at the browser's address bar confirmed the inclusion of a .onion domain, a clear sign that the website was part of this secretive and often dangerous network.

"What do we have here? Looks like someone's been a naughty boy," Dave murmured.

Without interacting with anything on the site, Dave scrolled down the page, taking in the content as he went. The website seemed to be a digital landfill, housing an assortment of illegal programs. From what Dave could see, there was a mixture of viruses listed, ranging from those stealthily collecting user information to ones capable of causing irreversible damage to infected systems. There was also an abundance of hacking programs designed to exploit various systems and programs.

The account's log revealed that the last activity had been the personal upload of an AI program devoid of any accompanying details as to what its purpose was. Just as he was about to click on the entry, the monitor went dark.

"Damn it," Dave muttered while crouching down to inspect the PC. It had shut down. Pressing the power button did nothing. Despite meticulously inspecting all the cables and plugs and attempting another restart, the computer remained unresponsive.

"Just my luck," Dave said with a heavy sigh of frustration.

He checked his watch again, 4:52 am. If he arranged the Digital Forensics Team and got the M.E. and CSI teams to contact him when they were done, then maybe he could grab a few hours of sleep before he had to go into the office.

Dialling the first of his calls as he walked back to the car, he exited the building and nodded at the still pale face of the police officer at the entrance. He was in his car, finishing up his last call to CSI, when the sharp, insistent beep of a message on his personal phone drew his attention.

"Now what?" he said, his voice tinged with growing frustration. All he wanted to do was crawl into bed and squeeze in what little rest he could.

Removing the phone from the glove box, he took a quick glance at the screen. The message was from an unfamiliar number, and it simply said,

Hello

Must be a wrong number, he thought to himself. Without a second thought, he tucked it into his pocket and set off on his way back home.

It took him thirty minutes to get there, and by the time he reached his front door, he could barely keep his eyes open. He dragged himself down the hallway towards his bedroom, only to be startled by the beeping of his phone.

Pulling it out of his pocket, he glanced at the screen and did a double take. On his way home, two messages had been sent to him, both of which had gone unnoticed.

Both messages came from the same unfamiliar

number as the first one. Two of them repeated the initial message, *Hello*. The one he had just received said,

> Hello Dave.

He paused in front of his bedroom door, gazing at it longingly before quickly typing out a response.

> Who is this?

Three dots appeared instantly, hovering on the screen a moment before the reply came through.

> Do you like monsters, Dave?

An icy chill shot down Dave's spine as he read the words. Sure, he'd told many of his friends and workmates about his hobby, but he had all of their numbers stored on his phone. This was from a new number. He supposed it could have been possible that one of them had bought a brand-new phone with a different number.

He tapped out a response.

> Whoever this is, it will need to wait. I've just come back from a crime scene and am about to grab a few hours sleep. Talk later.

He pocketed the phone and made a beeline for the bathroom to relieve himself. He was about to head to bed, exhausted and ready to collapse, when the message tone rang out again, breaking the silence. His anger rising, he yanked his phone out of his pocket and stared at the message in shock.

> You mean the one in apartment 223? I was there too.

Dave thought back to who he'd seen at the crime scene. There were only the three he'd met, the officer who he'd seen around the precinct a few times, Mark, the photographer, and Sam, the M.E. both of whom he'd worked alongside for a few years now. Could it be that the murderer sent the messages?

He typed out another reply.

> Is this Mark or Sam? Or are you the police officer I met before I went in?

Three dots immediately danced on the screen, yet no reply followed. Dave stood there for several minutes, staring at the phone screen expectantly, but there was no response.

"Screw this," he muttered to himself before he switched the phone off. Whoever it was could wait. Once he found out who was responsible, there would be hell to pay.

As soon as he collapsed into bed, exhaustion overtook him and he drifted off, but his slumber was short-lived as the shrill ring of the landline phone shattered the silence, startling him awake.

It rang again before he picked it up, expecting it to be a call related to the new case.

"Hello Dave, do you like monsters?"

Despite the obvious intention to frighten him, the cold, robotic, and monotone voice on the other end of the phone only sparked his anger, making his muscles stiffen and his veins pulsate with a burning rage.

"Listen, whoever this is, I'm going to kick your ass. I don't care who you are. When I find you, I'll make you sorry you were born. Now fuck off and leave me alone."

In a fit of rage, he slammed the handset down and ripped out the coiled cord that snaked from the back of the landline phone. Another thing he would have to deal with tomorrow, a landline phone replacement. He reached toward his work phone lying next to it and hesitated. He really should keep it on in case he got a legitimate call, but he was exhausted. Deciding to risk it, he turned it off before settling back down into bed, drifting off almost immediately into unconsciousness.

"Hello Dave."

Every room in his house seemed to reverberate with the cold, robotic words, as if they were emanating from every electronic device within, incessantly repeating, beating against his skull. Dave covered his ears with his hands, trying to keep the deafening roar of the words at bay, but to no avail. With fury, Dave ripped out everything plugged into the wall and hurled any battery-operated devices he could find onto the floor, but it was no use. The words seemed to scream from the very walls themselves, slipping through the gaps between his fingers that were clasped over his ears, almost as if they were desperate to be heard. Dave tried to drown out the sound with his screams, but it proved futile. Nothing helped. The volume increased, and blood began to pour from his ears. It grew louder still, the relentless sound drilling into his mind and pounding against the walls of his skull. Blood poured out of his ears, his nose, and then his pores, building up immense pressure until his head detonated like a melon, leaving behind a cloud of pink mist.

Dave jolted awake, with his heart pounding and a scream on his lips. His body dripped with sweat, saturating the bedsheets beneath him. He reached for the glass of water on his nightstand and downed it in one go.

"Hello Dave, I like your monsters."

Dave froze, with the glass still pressed to his lips. He slowly lowered the glass and placed it back on the nightstand before turning his head towards the foot of the bed, where an imposing shadow loomed motionless.

"Wh... who are you?"

"I'm your bugbear, Dave. Don't you recognise me?"

The sound of the monotone, robotic voice sent shivers down his spine, but he mustered the courage to reach out and switch on the lamp. The blinding glare of the light overwhelmed Dave's groggy eyes. He shielded his eyes with his hand and strained to see the end of the bed.

Sure enough, it was the bugbear. It stood there, stock still and silent, its artificial eyes seeming to stare directly at him.

"Who are you?" Dave repeated, scooting backwards against the headboard of his bed. "What do you want?"

The beast stood there, its silence filling the air with an eerie stillness. Suddenly, it lunged at him, its massive paws raised, the lamplight reflecting off the sharp, metallic claws Dave had painstakingly designed.

"You Dave. I want you."

In a desperate attempt, Dave reached for the drawer, only to feel his arm go limp at the monster's assault. Its metallic claws dug deep into his shoulder, mercilessly rending his flesh and leaving it hanging by a few tenuous threads. Blood coated the floor and walls from Dave's ruined shoulder as he writhed in pain.

The sudden trauma left him paralyzed, his body unable to move as the monster pressed its attack, its claws tearing into him, blood and gore sent flying with each strike.

His last vision was of the giant spider, demon, werewolf and zombie animatronic monstrosities trudging toward the bedroom to join in the slaughter before he fell into the infinite dark. By the time they were done, all that remained of his body was a heap of steaming organs on the bed. The monstrous figures surrounded it in silence, their forms stilled once more, their limbs stained with crimson.

Clay raised his hands toward the ceiling, feeling the stretch in his muscles and following it up with a couple of neck stretches. The wheels of his chair squeaked in protest as he pushed it away from the desk, rising to his feet and embarking on a lap around the Digital Forensics Lab to relieve the stiffness in his legs.

He had been studying the algorithm of the AI program uploaded to the dark web by the victim Nathan Roberts for hours, unravelling its complex logic, waving farewell to his colleagues as they left one by one until he was the only one left in the lab. The victim had programmed it to discover the weakness of any system it was uploaded to and exploit it for the purpose of the uploader. It had the potential to be used for any number of things: blackmail, intimidation, stealing information, impersonation, and even murder.

Nathan had made one crucial error in its development, however. He had made it so intelligent that it had started modifying its own programming as it learned. It had grown almost a will of its own and had developed its own defense mechanisms. It knew Nathan had the ability to terminate it and so it made sure he didn't have the chance, taking control of his collection of drones to lethal effect.

Once Detective Dave Calahan came into the picture, it knew he was the next biggest threat and so it used his hobby, the animatronic beasts, against him.

Fortunately, Clay's weightlifting hobby was not something that could be exploited as a vulnerability.

Still, he needed to be careful. The AI had adapted in ways that Clay hadn't been able to get a handle on just yet. He had put safeguards in place, which would be enough to protect him, but one slip-up could spell disaster.

The phone in his pocket started vibrating. Likely a message from his wife asking him when he was coming home. He was already late by a few hours.

His phone vibrated again. Then again. Then it was nonstop as messages continually flooded his phone.

"What the hell?"

Clay pulled out his phone, his fingers trembling as he scrolled through the messages, his face growing paler as he read each one.

His wife:

> What the hell Clay? My sister? Really? Don't bother coming home.

His boss:

> I don't know what the hell possessed you to send pictures like that, but you and I are going to have a little chat tomorrow morning.

His mother:

> Clay, I'm so disappointed in you. How could you do something so cruel?

"No... No, no no no no..."

Clay's face glistened with sweat as he logged back into his computer. The AI had somehow bypassed his security wall. It had infiltrated every aspect of his digital life, from his email to his phone and bank account. Not only was it sending messages to his contacts, but it was also using personal and compromising photos he had taken to make each message more targeted and malicious. His life was effectively ruined.

Stunned, Clay sat motionless as the screen before him went dark, leaving only two words in its center.

Hello Clay

One Night in Halloween Land

Chase waved to his last client of the day as she exited the gym. A flirtatious smile over her shoulder and the suggestive swaying of her hips, her only response.

Chase shook his head with a smile and checked his watch. He had thirty minutes to spare before he needed to leave to get to Halloween Land.

In his late twenties, Chase had a toned body that suited his profession yet was not overly muscular. With his attractive chiselled face and jet-black hair to complete the picture, he was the envy of many and a sought-after personal trainer.

Already in his exercise clothes, he loaded up his program for the day, beginning a quick workout. Not as thorough as his usual one, he still completed most of his routine before he had to finish, gathering his gym bag and heading to the changing room for a shower.

Feeling refreshed, Chase grabbed his car keys from

the office and, with a nod and a quick goodbye to Jean, the gym manager, he headed to his car, eager to get on his way.

Every year Chase had left his Halloween decorating to the last minute. Although he had sworn this year to do it earlier, the hectic schedule he had over the last few weeks made that task impossible. He wasn't complaining, though. When he had started, it was a struggle to get any clients at all, a stark contrast to these days where he can barely keep up. It was great for the bank account, at least. Already visualizing what he was going to buy at the store, he couldn't help but smile, feeling his excitement grow. He enjoyed Halloween and had always made sure his house looked appropriately spooky for the kids to enjoy. Who was he kidding? He chuckled to himself. It was more for him than it was for them.

At least living alone had its perks. After breaking up with his long-term girlfriend, Julie, a few months ago after he had discovered her cheating on him, Chase had initially sunk into a depressive state. After a few days mired in self-misery, he had pulled himself together and put all his focus on work to keep busy, and it had paid off. Now that time had passed, he enjoyed the quiet and the freedom of doing whatever he wanted, and what he wanted this year was to make a display that was the envy of his street.

He switched on his left indicator and turned down a gravel road off the main street of Jackson, his local town. The road was bumpy and uneven, reflecting the lack of maintenance in this sparsely populated area, where farmsteads were the primary dwellings. The countryside transformed into sprawling paddocks as he passed by, filled with gently swaying wheat stalks and livestock.

Here also was Halloween Land. A former old farmstead turned into a Halloween superstore of sorts, now housing the latest in decorations and animatronics. It had become something of a tourist attraction, which wasn't surprising, as there wasn't anything noteworthy otherwise in Jackson.

Chase pulled into the car park, found a spot and checked his watch - 1 pm. 'Perfect,' he thought. 'I'll spend a few hours here and still have plenty of time at home to put everything together.'

Exiting the car, Chase approached the entrance to Halloween Land.

Set in a clearing surrounded by lush bushland, the store had an atmosphere perfectly suited for the spooky season. The rickety building he approached lent itself to an eerie air, the various decorations and creative displays enhancing the atmosphere. A prominent neon sign next to the entrance sign stated, "Enter if you dare". Solid stone gargoyles with painted bloody teeth sat on both sides of the door as if to guard the horrors contained within. Displays of animatronic monsters surrounded the veranda, another sign directing customers to the back of the ramshackle building where it promised yet more mechanized monsters and outdoor displays to entice customers.

Knowing what he wanted to buy, Chase wasted no time in heading to the back of the building. He quickly chose a few horrors from the array of monstrosities, including an animatronic crawling zombie, a dancing pumpkin thing, a pirate skeleton with glowing red eyes, and a fortune teller hovering over a crystal ball.

Heading toward the counter to pay, he took some more time to browse through the store and chose a few more pieces to enhance his display, adding them to his bill. When he was ready to leave, the store owner collected Chase's new treasures and brought them out in a trolley so Chase could transport them to the car.

Just as he was about to wheel his trolley toward the exit, he felt a tapping on his shoulder, a desperate voice accompanying it. Turning around, he saw an older blonde-haired lady, her face creased with anxiety, rubbing the back of her neck.

"Sorry, I normally wouldn't ask this, but I'm running short of time. Are you able to help me with moving these to my van?" she asked, pointing at the stone gargoyles near the entrance. Chase looked to the store owner for confirmation and, getting it via a nod, said, "Sure" with a warm smile at the lady.

"You're a lifesaver, thank you!" she said, her face softening with relief. "My van is parked just at the side."

Leaving the store, they approached the van, and she opened the rear doors.

"If you can just lift them in here for me, I can get my son to help get them out when I get home."

"No problem," Chase said, selecting a trolley and positioning it underneath one of the gargoyles, hoisting it and wheeling it towards the van.

Taking off his jacket so as not to risk ruining it when he lifted the gargoyle, he folded and placed it on a stone bench positioned next to the side of the store. With a grunt of effort, he lifted the gargoyle into the van, getting a horn caught on his shirt, the audible tearing of fabric justifying the removal of his jacket.

Turning to retrieve the second one, he felt a breeze tease the hairs on his chest from the newly exposed hole in his shirt. 'I was due for a new shirt anyway,' Chase thought to himself with a wry smile.

After getting the second one in the van without further incident, the lady shook his hand gratefully. She expressed her thanks once more and insisted on paying for his ruined shirt, a kind gesture he politely declined.

As he waved goodbye, he made his way back to his trolley and glanced at his watch - it was 4 pm. 'Perfect, still plenty of time for decorating,' he thought to himself, feeling his spirits rise at the thought. Pushing the trolley towards his car, he noticed a sudden movement out of the corner of his eye by the animatronic displays at the back of the store. Spotting a couple of scarecrows he hadn't seen before, which were separated from the other monsters, he took a moment to admire them.

The scarecrows stood tall with their unkempt, dirty yellow straw hair and wore vibrant red button-up shirts. Tufts of straw poked out from the fabric, while loose-fitting pants were tied at the ankle with tattered ropes. They were each securely fastened to poles that had been driven into the ground. Their straw hands gripped a plastic mini chainsaw prop, its painted bloody blades adding a gruesome touch. Large green eyes were emphasized with red-painted eyelids, creating a bloody effect. Surrounding the nose and mouth was a thick, darkened beard, framing a large, menacing mouth that displayed peg-like teeth in a sadistic grin.

A breeze was ruffling the tufts of straw on the silent sentinels, which is what he assumed caught his eye. He shifted his gaze to the one furthest away, and as he studied its face, a frown creased his brow. There was something peculiar about its smile. It looked as if it could almost come to life at any moment.

He shrugged it off and carried on toward his car, loading in his newly gained decorations. An uneasy feeling of being watched crept over him. The hairs on his neck stood up and he glanced back over his shoulder at the scarecrow. It stood there as before, with the same creepy smile plastered on its face. Conscious of the time, he tore his gaze away from the thing and finished his loading before he slid into his car and set off on his way home.

He pulled into his driveway thirty minutes later, relieved to be home. After unloading the car, he started setting up the house, readying it for the night ahead.

He started by draping police tape, complete with bloodstains and handprints, diagonally across the door. To enhance the door's appearance, he added more adhesive blood prints, crafting a grotesque motif. The hedge surrounding his house became a canvas for fake spiderwebs, with strategically placed plastic spiders adding to the spooky vibe.

On either side of the path leading to his front door, he placed carved pumpkins that he had prepared the night before. Each pumpkin had a lit candle inside, casting a haunting glow in the fading sunlight. Next, he looped a hanging plastic body within a burlap sack around the lowest hanging branch of the tree in his front yard and secured it several feet above the ground. Afterwards, he placed foam gravestones throughout the yard around the tree. Finally, he placed and set up his animatronic displays amongst them and tested them to ensure they were working as intended.

Standing on his porch, he surveyed his work with a sense of satisfaction, hands planted on his hips. After making some further adjustments to positioning, he was satisfied, and he headed inside to change into his blood-covered police costume and prepare the candy in a large decorative plastic bowl.

The time was approaching 6 pm when he switched on the TV and prepared to sit down, when a knock on the door signaled his first trick-or-treaters of the night.

Donning his police cap, and with a baton and candy bowl in hand, he opened the door with a smile to a gaggle of excited voices. Werewolves, mummies, undead pirates, witches, warlocks, banshees, and demonic beings soon filled the path to his door. One after the other, they made their way back and forth from the street filled with excited children and bored parents, some stopping to study his display as impatient parents and siblings called out to them to hurry on to the next house.

As the night wore on and the stream of children

dwindled, Chase ran out of his last batch of candy and closed the door for the last time with a satisfied sigh. Halloween was now done for another year.

With a yawn and a stretch, Chase happily placed the police cap on the nearby coat rack and went in search of his phone. He had been so engrossed in taking care of the trick-or-treaters that he had forgotten all about dinner. His stomach was now making him aware of that fact.

Retrieving the phone from his bedroom, he sat on the couch, browsing through the various fast-food options still open. Finding a suitable one, he patted his pockets for his wallet, only to find it wasn't on him. Heading upstairs, he searched through the clothes he had worn prior to changing. Then, with a groan, it dawned on him that he had left it in his jacket pocket. The very same jacket he had left behind on the stone bench at Halloween Land.

"Oh no," he groaned to himself, feeling a sinking sensation in his stomach when he realized he had no choice but to go back to the store and retrieve it.

With a sigh, he changed out of his costume and back into his regular clothes. He grabbed his keys, opened and locked the front door behind him, and jumped into his car. As he drove away, he noticed the streets were now almost empty, with only a few stragglers left still trying to eke out the last of the candy from houses still willing to part with it.

The pitch-black darkness of the night lent itself to an eerie air as lights from houses became sparse the further he traveled, the frivolity of the night left behind with the fading signs of civilization. Upon finally arriving at the Halloween Land turnoff, he pulled up and parked his vehicle in front of the closed store.

In the darkness, the rickety structure loomed before him, the car headlights casting eerie shadows that evoked images of a scene from a horror movie. The dense bush-land and looming trees felt like they were closing in from either side as he turned off the headlights and stepped out of the car.

Using his phone's flashlight, he made his way to the stone bench at the side of the building, the sound of his footsteps echoing through the quiet of the night.

Spotting his jacket on the bench, he let out a sigh of relief, grateful to find his wallet still safely tucked inside. He put it on, patting the pocket to ensure his wallet was still in place, and turned back towards his car.

Moving forward, he felt something soft give way under his foot, causing a wet squelch to echo through the air. Lifting it quickly, he saw what looked like strands of clotted blood fall from the bottom of his shoe. The beam of the torchlight swung downward, and a horrified gasp escaped his lips when it revealed the remnants of a fore-arm, the hand barely clinging on by thin strands of flesh.

"This can't be real," he muttered to himself, his voice filled with disbelief. "This must be a decoration that someone dropped. Yes, that must be it," he chuckled quietly, feeling a mix of nervousness and relief.

He left it there and headed to his car, eager to get home, order food, and relax for the rest of the night.

A sudden crashing sound from the direction of the

store behind him suddenly halted his steps. Startled, he spun around, the beam from the phone illuminating the broken and listing door as it clung precariously to the one remaining hinge at the entrance to Halloween Land.

More crashing sounds came from deeper in the store, accompanied by the sound of shattering glass as something forged a path of destruction through the store aisles.

Chase switched off the flashlight and took a step back, dialing 911 on his phone, praying that he hadn't drawn any attention from the person inside. After a few seconds of silence, he lowered his phone and noticed the words 'No Signal' displayed on the screen.

"Of course," he muttered under his breath, his voice filled with exasperation.

As he made his way towards the doorway, a groan resonated from the store, prompting him to switch on the phone flashlight. The air felt heavy with tension as he cautiously moved forward.

"Hello?" he called out cautiously. Another groan, this time fainter than before. "I'm coming in," he announced anxiously, inching his way toward the entrance, ears straining for any further sign of danger.

Inside, he came to a stop and swept the store with the phone's flashlight, his eyes on high alert for any signs of movement. Finding none, he advanced further into the store. The glow of the flashlight revealed broken shelving and various Halloween party decor, tableware, lighting, props, and ornaments in pieces scattered across the floor.

The trail of destruction led towards the back, where the cash register was located.

Moving down the aisle, he paused in terror at the sudden popping of a shattered globe beneath his foot; the sound reverberating sharply around the room. He froze, his muscles tense, and held his breath, straining to catch any sound of a reaction. The store was silent, as if waiting with bated breath alongside him. Gradually, after a few moments, he relaxed, shifting the phone's flashlight towards his foot, making sure to avoid the string of decorated pumpkin lights that had been knocked to the floor.

Reaching the end of the aisle, he looked around cautiously. Overturned costumes and hangers littered the floor near the cash register, along with shattered glass from the window immediately behind it. With a sudden gust of wind, raindrops started to splatter onto the vacant counter before him, adding to the unsettling atmosphere.

Stepping behind the counter, he froze, his face draining of color as he took in the broken body of the shopkeeper sprawled on the floor. The shopkeeper was barely recognizable, his limbs twisted in a grisly display and folded in half, positioned as if he were an animatronic himself, ready to be manipulated into a position of choosing. Pools of blood surrounded the traumatized body. Chase took a step back, his heart racing as a sudden groan shattered his stunned reverie. Leaning down, he pressed his ear against the man's mouth and heard faint, shallow breaths.

The man let out another pained groan before forcing

his heavy eyelids to open, revealing bloodshot eyes. "Rooooo," the man gasped, his terror-stricken eyes darting towards Chase. "Roooooon," the man tried again, his breath now raspy and barely discernible. "Roooonaldo," with one last word and a ragged breath, the man fell silent.

"Ronaldo?" Chase repeated under his breath. The sudden flash of lightning outside the broken window, followed by a peal of thunder, briefly filled the shop with light, revealing a row of animatronic monsters lining the inside of the hall behind the cash register which led to the back door and the display yard.

The menacing shadows of the animatronics seemed to converge on Chase, prompting him to turn his gaze toward the closest one. It was one of the scarecrows he had caught a glimpse of as he was leaving earlier that afternoon.

The store was plunged back into darkness as the fleeting glow from the lightning disappeared. Chase's hands grew clammy as he aimed his phone flashlight at the thing, desperately backing up in fear.

The scarecrow was covered in splatters of blood, the gruesome presentation of its clothing and its face magnified by the drips of blood and chunks of flesh falling from the small chainsaw it was holding. The grin on its face widened, the green eyes now alive and filled with menace as it deliberately unhooked itself from the stand it was attached to, taking its first steps toward Chase.

Panicking, Chase sprinted toward the entrance, only to stumble over the tangled string of lights lying on the floor. He reached out to the shelf nearby to steady himself, but his desperate grasp only resulted in it crashing down on top of him. With desperation, he shoved at the shelving, finally managing to move it slightly and wriggle himself out from underneath. Just as he did so, he could feel the scarecrow's bony, straw-like fingers close around his ankle, pulling him with ease toward it.

His arms scrambled for something to use as a weapon as he slid backward, grabbing at a plastic sword that had fallen out of a container of prop weapons. The grip on his ankle released before he could use it and he turned over to see the thing standing over him, the chainsaw it held roaring to life as it pulled the starter cord, the teeth of the chainsaw spitting blood and viscera, the aftermath of its attack on the store owner.

Slashing the sword in desperation, Chase landed a blow on the arm of the scarecrow. The momentum of the blow loosened its grip on the chainsaw, and the scarecrow staggered sideways into a stack of plastic Halloween pumpkins, sending them scattering.

Using his hands to back up and then turning and rising to his feet, he dashed out of the exit and sprinted towards his car; the rain driving into his face as he fumbled for the keys. Unlocking the door in haste, he slid into the driver's seat and started the car, the engine roaring to life as if it were as desperate to get away as he was. The moment Chase shifted the car into reverse and pressed the accelerator, the front windshield imploded, showering him with tiny, sharp fragments of safety glass.

With a cry, Chase was forcefully dragged through the window, the sharp glass shards slicing into his flesh as he glided over the car's bonnet and crashed onto the ground, the impact reverberating through his body.

His eyes snapped wide in horror. Instinct took over, and he rolled aside as the chainsaw screamed past, slicing into the bonnet behind him with a metallic shriek. The acrid scent of scorched steel filled his nostrils. Above him, the scarecrow twisted violently, its limbs jerking as it wrestled with the jammed blade. Groaning metal echoed, sharp and uneven, like the car itself was crying out. Chase, his heart racing, pushed himself up and scrambled back toward the shop. He recalled the shed he had spotted earlier that day in the shop's backyard and ran in that direction, desperate to seek refuge.

He could hear eerie cackling laughter coming from behind, intermingled with the unsettling sound of straw lightly slapping against the wet ground as it chased after him, its gait as awkward as the scarecrow itself. He reached the shed door and grabbed and twisted the knob, hoping it hadn't been locked. Thankfully, it swung open without any resistance. Darting inside, he slammed it shut, sliding the lock in place, and leaned against it, trying to catch his breath as he took in his surroundings.

The sound of a light tapping on the door behind him caused Chase to swiftly distance himself from it. He noticed a window nearby and hurried over to it, hoping to get a better view of the creature. Peering out, he saw the scarecrow's wide grin as it playfully knocked on the door, giving him a wave in a creepy caricature of a greeting.

The scarecrow's smile faded into a frown of disappointment, almost as if it had expected Chase to open it. It persisted in knocking on the door, its unsettling focus on him never wavering.

In an instant, the beaming grin returned, and it took a step back, thrusting the roaring chainsaw menacingly towards the door. Chase realized it was toying with him, the thing relishing the game it was playing.

The sound of the chainsaw biting into the door echoed through the space, filling Chase with a sense of urgency as he scanned his surroundings for a weapon.

The walls were adorned with a collection of antique farming tools, each one weathered and covered in rust. None of them looked to be in working order. He could feel the vibrations from the chainsaw behind him as it continued to slice into the door. It would only be a matter of time before the scarecrow broke through.

Chase's gaze locked onto a shelf lined with power tools, most appearing serviceable. He plunged his hands into the clutter, shoving aside anything inadequate, his desperation mounting as he searched for one that would do the job. The chainsaw's roar intensified behind him, its vibrations shaking the implements on the wall. After sifting through almost all the tools, he finally spotted the one he needed. A chainsaw. With shaking hands, he yanked the starter cord. The engine responded with a series of sputters but failed to catch. With a resounding crash, the shed door behind him gave way, falling into two distinct pieces on the floor. Chase's frustration grew as he pulled on the cord, uttering a curse. He gave it one last powerful tug, pushing the throttle to full speed, and the engine sprang to life with a guttural roar.

Chase turned in time to see the scarecrow swing at him. The creature held its chainsaw high, the sharp teeth glistening as a lightning flash illuminated the room through the open door. Temporarily blinded, Chase lurched aside but wasn't quick enough to avoid the jagged teeth of the chainsaw as they shredded through the fabric of his clothes, hacking into his collarbone and tearing it from the hands of the scarecrow.

With a pained howl, Chase collapsed to the ground, wrenching the chainsaw out of his flesh. He quickly crawled behind the bench, clutching his own chainsaw in a tight grip, trying to create some distance for himself. As he got back on his feet, he covered the wound with his hand, desperate to stem the bleeding. Looking down at it, he could see the crimson blood trickling through his trembling fingers. He knew he had only a limited amount of time before he lost strength from blood loss.

The clatter of power tools falling to the floor spurred him into action as the scarecrow swiped its arms across the bench to get to him. Backing away, he took a moment to consider his options. As the pain intensified, his left arm grew increasingly numb. The daunting prospect of driving a stick shift car with only one functioning arm, let alone even making it to the damn thing, all the while being chased by a monster that would more than likely outrun him, seemed like an impossible feat. His only option was to fight back and pray for a stroke of luck that would allow him to take it out.

With a sudden leap, the scarecrow cleared the bench and landed gracefully beside him. It retrieved its discarded chainsaw, its teeth fresh with Chase's blood, and swung once again, but Chase evaded the attack. Reacting quickly, he raised his own chainsaw and cut into the scarecrow's right arm as it spun by, effortlessly slicing through the straw-like substance. As the arm hit the ground, wisps of smoke rose from it, accompanied by a piercing scream from the thing as it crashed to the floor. Chase couldn't look away from the smoking limb, mesmerized by the astonishing transformation of the straw-like surface into a repulsive, black, and slimy exterior, complete with what appeared to be rows of serrated teeth.

"What the…" Chase exclaimed, tearing his eyes away from the morphed limb to focus on the monster before him. It slowly rose to its feet, newly formed flesh knitting around its shoulder as a new limb started to develop. Its tentacle-like tendril extended outward and whipped around in a display of agitation, sharp serrated teeth appearing on its surface like the now discarded limb lying limp on the floor. As the new appendage whipped toward him, he could feel the teeth sink into his leg, immediately gripping his calf and yanking him off balance, sending him crashing to the ground.

Screaming in pain, Chase thrashed on the floor, trying to loosen the vice-like grip the teeth had on him. Realizing he still had the chainsaw, he hacked at the tentacle, the teeth of the blade catching and cutting into it halfway through before it let go of his leg and retreated toward the monster, leaving behind a trail of ichor in its wake.

Behind the writhing entity, Chase's eyes locked onto a wood-chipping machine, its sharp blades glinting in the dim light. Through the haze of pain radiating from his shattered collarbone, a plan took shape. Gritting his teeth, he charged at the monster, each movement sending a fresh jolt of agony through his body. His grip tightened around the chainsaw, its weight almost unbearable, but he forced it forward, aiming for the scarecrow thing's midsection. The chainsaw let out a high-pitched whine as the blade tore into it, driving it backwards. Ichor and black liquid shot toward Chase's face, the viscous substance stinging his eyes as it made contact. Frantically rubbing his eyes, he cleared his vision just enough to see that he had successfully cornered the monster against the wood chipper. The impact of their collision left it momentarily stunned, its anguished screeches echoing birdlike in the space.

Before it could recover, Chase swung the chainsaw at the monster's head, causing the straw-like material to disintegrate into chunks of black flesh that scattered with every blow. The scarecrow flailed at Chase in desperation, its tentacle-like limbs wrapping around Chase's waist, teeth once again biting into him and attempting to pull him away. Chase clenched his teeth, feeling the sharp pain coursing through his body, as he forcefully drove the chainsaw into the thing's head, leaving it dangling precariously over the gaping maw of the wood chipper and the jagged metal teeth that awaited below.

In a last-ditch effort, Chase lunged towards the switch, his entire body quivering with desperation. With a satisfying click, he turned it on, and the once dormant engine roared to life, filling the shed with its deafening noise. The monster's head was sucked into the machine, causing a violent explosion of vile liquid that splattered the walls and covered Chase, its nauseating smell overpowering the air.

Sliding onto the floor, his back against the shed wall, Chase delicately unraveled the clinging suckers and squirming tentacles wrapped tightly around his body, letting out pained gasps as chunks of his flesh came free along with the embedded teeth.

With urgency, he tore his tattered shirt and jacket into makeshift bandages, cinching them tightly around his waist and collarbone to stop the blood flow. Completely drained, he slumped over in exhaustion.

Lying lifeless against the wood chipper, the monster's body began to emit wisps of foul-smelling smoke, as it morphed into the same slimy black texture as its tentacle arm. The clothing it had worn slid off its transformed form as it collapsed into a shapeless black mass on the ground. With great effort, Chase wearily rose to his feet, his body throbbing with pain, and started limping toward the exit. Outside, the rain was alive with bursts of lightning, casting an ethereal glow as Chase let it wash away the heat and discomfort from his skin and eyes.

At last, he reached the car, easing himself behind the

wheel with shaking limbs. He barely managed to start the engine before the darkness overtook him. One final heartbeat pulsed through his chest—then silence, as both he and Halloween passed at the chime of midnight.

Beyond the shed, a pair of vivid green eyes observed the scene, a malicious grin adorning a face that slowly shifted its gaze back towards the forest, leaving traces of straw behind with each step as it disappeared into the shadows.

Inside Halloween Land, an animatronic scarecrow of the same likeness lay face down on the floor, a blood-stained price tag attached. Ronaldo $99.95.

Storm of Shadows

Mary hummed to herself as she approached the antique front door she had convinced her husband, Paul, to install. She stood before it for a moment, admiring its workmanship, a relic from a bygone era. The frilly white short sheer curtains covering the glass shimmered in the lightning flashes from outside. She made sure the door was locked before continuing her rounds, inspecting each door and window. It was a ritual she'd maintained since they'd settled into the aged yet sturdy single-story house.

It was a cold and stormy night, unusual for this time of the year. Outside, the wind howled like a mournful spirit, its anguished cry seeping through the walls, twisting the silence inside into something uneasy and restless. Rain lashed against the windows, the droplets racing down the glass like tears. The house creaked and groaned, as if burdened by the storm's pressing weight.

Mary finished her rounds and made her way toward

her son's bedroom, hoping he hadn't been awakened by the raging storm outside.

Adam, a bright, energetic fourteen-year-old, was the center of her universe. He had always been a mummy's boy and, despite now being a teenager, he remained so; something she was grateful for. She had always feared that as he grew older, he would naturally become closer to Paul and drift away from her, but that hadn't happened so far. Nevertheless, she held onto every precious day with him, aware that his journey to adulthood would eventually pull them apart.

Careful not to add to the sound of the storm battering the house, she tiptoed past the creaky floorboards in the hallway and peeked through the open door of Adam's room. He was fast asleep and nestled snugly under the covers, with an extra winter blanket draped over the top for added warmth.

She studied his face, suddenly aware of how grown up he was looking. His face was gradually shedding its baby fat, revealing the emergence of defined cheekbones. His facial hair was growing more these days too, still soft but on its way to becoming the coarse stubble of an adult. She let out a sigh, realizing how quickly time had passed. It had seemed like just yesterday when she had held baby Adam in her arms.

The window next to his bed caught her attention as a flash of lightning illuminated the room, penetrating the closed curtains. The echoing boom of thunder that ensued caused Adam to stir and change his position in bed, but he remained asleep. The brief flash of light in the darkness was enough to reveal a partially concealed board that had been shoved under the bed in obvious haste. With a furrowed brow, she approached it, bending down to get a closer look, careful not to make a sound. It was an old Ouija board, its surface scuffed and faded but still readable. A metal planchette, elaborately decorated, lay beside it.

As she stood, her gaze flicked between Adam and the Ouija board. She would need to talk to him tomorrow, make sure he understood that this wasn't just another idle pastime. Teenagers were naturally curious, drawn to the thrill of the unknown, but the board wasn't like the horror movies made it out to be. It wasn't a game. It was a tether—a bridge between the living and whatever lurked beyond. And once that bridge was crossed, there was no telling what might follow him back.

Leaving his room with a concerned frown, she walked towards the study, where a dimly lit lamp cast a gentle glow, visible through the partially open doorway. Slipping through the gap, her eyes fell upon Paul, engrossed in his work on the computer. His work had consumed a lot of his time lately. He had picked up a lot of commissions at the digital art conference he had recently come back from. Since then, he'd hurled himself into his work, determined to build a career and build up their savings for the family's future.

Clicking away from his work, Paul opened a photo and leaned back in his chair. He let out a deep, sorrowful sigh, his breath hitching as he fought to hold back tears. Mary snuck closer in curiosity and halted in confusion. It was a photo capturing a precious moment of together-ness, with her, Paul, and Adam all huddled together, Adam caught in the middle of laughter while Mary and Paul looked at him with adoring eyes.

The photo had been taken just last year, capturing the joyous end-of-year celebration of Adam's basketball team, with one of the parents behind the camera. Adam had steadfastly refused to smile until Paul had stepped in and relentlessly tickled him until he couldn't help but break into laughter, resulting in a perfectly timed picture.

She was about to ask him what was wrong when a piercing, eerie wail echoed through the doorway. At first, Mary mistook the sound for the howling wind outside, but as she listened more closely, she realized it was some-thing else entirely. Suddenly, the sound ceased. It almost felt as if whatever was behind the sound was trying out its voice for the first time.

Mary looked at Paul, who remained seated at the desk, unable to look away from the photo. Tears streamed down his face as he tried to suppress his quiet sobbing. It seemed as though he hadn't heard the sound. Was she imagining things? She shivered, feeling a heavy sense of foreboding. There was a distinct sense of unease in the house, a feeling of wrongness that seemed to permeate the air.

She approached the gap in the office door and peeked through it toward the living room, but from this vantage point, there was nothing she could see besides the faint outline of the sofa at the end of the hallway.

As if on cue, the haunting wailing began again,

causing an immediate shiver to run down her spine and covering her exposed skin with goosebumps. The sound was dissonant, an otherworldly sound that rose in volume until it was joined by a cacophony of whispers and screams, a torrent of discordant voices full of pain and suffering, with the promise of more to come. Her eyes widened with terror as she retreated from the door, seeking safety in the corner of the room. She felt an overwhelming urge to run, but there was nowhere for her to go.

"Paul!" she cried out, her voice sharp with panic, but he didn't seem to hear her. Maybe the sound was drowning her out, or maybe she was too frozen with fear to speak louder than a whisper. Paul remained at his desk, still sobbing and showing no sign of reaction as he reached for a tissue next to his monitor, wiping at his puffy eyes.

The sound stopped once again. Mary strained her ears, trying to catch any hint of movement in the living room, but all she could hear was the ferocity of the wind and the pounding rain from the storm outside. The rain relentlessly beat against the windows as the wind continued to howl without pause. Each crack of thunder reverberated through the walls, accompanied by blinding flashes of lightning.

Suddenly, a blood-curdling scream from Adam's room pierced the air. It was a scream of pure terror, a desperate cry for help that sent Paul scrambling to his feet and rushing from the office toward Adam's room. In his rush, he didn't even seem to notice her pressed against the corner as he ran past. She gathered herself and followed his rapidly fading footsteps. Adam's scream continued, growing louder and more desperate, punctuated by his anguished pleas for Paul, which pierced Mary's heart.

Paul charged through the open doorway and came to an abrupt halt inside. Adam was still screaming, staring and pointing towards a chair with a blanket draped over it in the corner of his room next to his closet. No, the blanket wasn't draped, Mary realised as she entered the room. There was something there. A figure was huddling beneath it. The form shifted as it leaned forward, and Mary, despite her desire to protect her son, couldn't help but step backwards in horror when she saw a brief flash of otherworldly yellow eyes appear, then fade away. The howl that Mary had heard before in the office began to emanate from the cloaked figure, this time more menacing and haunting than before. Adam's screams intensified as he scrambled backward against the bedhead, trying to get as much distance from the thing as possible.

Paul looked in the direction of Adam's pointing finger towards the chair and saw only the blanket. He tried to yell over Adam's screams, assuring him that there was nothing there and he was just having a bad dream. He couldn't see it, Mary realised. Why couldn't he see it?

Mary tried calling out to Adam, trying to coax him out of the bed toward her, but it was as if he couldn't hear her. In an instant, the figure stood up, causing the blanket to drop and unveil something that couldn't possibly be. The thing appeared to be the perfect living embodiment of the devil. Covered in reddish muscular skin, the demon oozed menace. Every inch of its body promised pain and suffering for the unfortunate victim it turned its attention to. Its movements were predatory and uncanny, its eyes set into its angular horned head glowing with intensity and fixed only on the cowering form of Adam, who continued his uncontrollable screaming.

All Paul saw was the blanket lifting and then dropping onto the floor, but it was enough to frighten him into shouting for Adam to come to him. When Adam didn't, he rushed to the bed and tried to pull Adam toward him, but Adam instinctively hit out at him, his fight-or-flight response in full effect.

The demonic entity, wearing a sinister grin, reached the foot of the bed, relishing the palpable fear emanating from Adam. With slow, intentional steps, it advanced towards the head of the bed, where Adam and Paul were still struggling.

Mary's pleas to alert Paul and Adam fell on deaf ears as they continued on with their struggle, oblivious to her warnings. She set her sights on the demon. There was no way she would let anything touch her son. With this thought consuming her, she mustered the strength to suppress her fear and terror caused by the nightmarish thing, charging towards it and bringing it crashing down beside the bed.

Caught off guard, the demon's face contorted with a mixture of surprise and irritation as it struggled in her grasp. Its power was immense. As the initial surprise wore off, Mary could feel it moving around with ease underneath her. She exerted every ounce of her strength, wrapping her legs and arms around its body, determined to create a distraction and buy precious time for Adam and Paul to escape.

"M... Mom?" With a hesitant voice, Adam called out, his strained tone tinged with a touch of wonder and surprise.

As Paul pulled Adam closer, he could feel the boy's resistance fading away, his attention fixed on the chaos unfolding on the floor, where Mary was engaged in a fierce battle with the demon.

Paul lifted him up and turned toward the door and froze, his breath catching in his throat at the sight before him. Mary was locked in a desperate struggle with the demonic beast, both now horrifyingly visible. Her face contorted with panic, her arms straining to hold the thing at bay.

"Mary?" His voice cracked, the tone raw, shaken. "Honey?!"

Disbelief, horror, and adrenaline crashed together as he stepped forward, torn between shielding the boy in his arms and rushing to help her. Mary looked toward the pair, trying to warn them to stay back, her grip loosening for just a second. That second was all the demon needed. Seizing the opening with unnatural speed, it wrenched her arms away and viciously swiped at her chest with its razor-sharp claws, effortlessly carving through her body as though she were nothing more than an irritating pest to be eradicated.

Mary lay there, stunned. Strangely, there was no blood from the wound, but she felt a sudden immense loss of energy, as if the wound was mortal, regardless. Confused, she moved her hand over the gash, feeling nothing but a chilling emptiness as it passed through her chest. She shuddered involuntarily, and for a moment, she saw her body flicker, like a glitch in reality.

"Mom? No, I can't lose you again. Get up, Mom, get up!"

Adam sobbed, each breath a broken hymn as he stretched his hands toward her, yearning for her touch. Overwhelmed with shock, Paul fell to his knees, clutching Adam tightly against him, tears streaming down his face as he locked eyes with Mary.

The demon's presence loomed as it neared the pair. Hovering above them, it paused, its intense stare directed at them, its lips parting to reveal its teeth, glimmering like polished blades.

When Mary saw the shocked expressions on Adam and Paul's faces, she knew something was terribly wrong. She had no idea what was happening to her, but she couldn't let the demon take her son. She lifted herself to her elbows as her energy levels continued to plummet and realized that, whatever was happening to her, she had little time left. Her gaze locked onto the metal planchette glinting beneath the bed. She reached for it, fingers trembling—and the moment they touched its cold surface, memories crashed over her like a tide.

It was a dark and stormy night, much like tonight. She was driving along a remote road, rain pelting the windscreen as the wipers fought to clear the torrent of water rushing down from above. Fog drifted a meter from the ground, covering the fields on either side of her and the road in front. She rubbed her eyes, feeling an overwhelming sense of fatigue. She had been coming back from a sales conference, but the exact location seemed to escape her memory. She knew only that it had been a long night, and she was eager to get home. There was a brief flash, and her eyes were now focused on the speedometer, showing the speed far above what it should be for these conditions. Another brief flash to sometime later. She was struggling to keep her eyes open. Another flash, she was drifting off the road. Flash, she was headed directly into the path of a cluster of trees. Another flash, no vision, just the sound of crunching metal and glass.

The next thing she remembered was tonight, walking toward the front door to check the lock. Then she looked down at the planchette and the Ouija board, and a sudden understanding washed over her. She had died that night on the road. Adam must have reached out through the board, hoping to contact her. But instead, he cracked the veil. Something else had slipped through, drawn to the invitation like rot to a wound.

Using every ounce of strength she had left, she hauled herself back to her feet and staggered toward the towering form of the demon. Fixated on its prey, the demon remained oblivious to Mary's presence until the very last moment, whirling around in surprise as she approached. With one last effort, Mary launched herself at it with a desperate cry. She thrust the planchette into its neck as the demon's claws tore into her chest, deepening her wound.

The two stood for a moment, their bodies intertwined in a celestial embrace, a timeless clash of good and evil, with neither emerging victorious. Mary had time for one last parting smile, her eyes brimming with love, as she mouthed, "I love you" to both her husband and son. Then the two figures drifted apart, disappearing into thin air. Adam and Paul clung to each other, tears streaming down their faces, as the planchette fell with a loud clatter onto the floor.

Six months later

"Here you go," Paul said, hefting a large cardboard box from the moving truck and dumping it into Adam's waiting arms. "Be useful for once and take this one down to the basement for me," he said, slapping Adam on the back with a mischievous grin.

"Why is it always me that has to go down into the creepy basement?" Adam groaned, turning toward the path leading to their new house.

"Just lucky, I guess. Now get going," Paul said with a grin, turning back to climb into the bed of the truck to grab the next box.

With an irritated sigh, Adam trudged up the concrete steps that led to the front door.

After Adam and Paul had lost Mary in a car accident eighteen months ago, Paul had thrown himself further into work to distract himself from drowning in grief. It had paid off far better than expected. Even though the incident six months ago still weighed on both Adam and Paul, they had found comfort in one another and rebuilt the communication that had been lacking ever since Mary's accident. The pair had decided to move on from their house, the only one Adam had ever known, to begin anew. Things had accelerated from that point on, and now they stood before a breathtaking double-story house in a neighboring town. It was a place they hoped would be the start of an exciting new chapter in their lives.

Adam grumbled to himself as he entered through the front door and stomped down the hallway toward the basement door, set into the wall beneath the stairs leading to the second floor. With the box's weight shifted to one arm, he gripped the doorknob and pulled it open. The eerie groan of the hinges made him wince, reminding him of the doors to haunted basements in horror films. Adam rolled his eyes; he would need to remind his dad to oil the hinges before he went down again. Flicking on the light, he descended the stairs and unceremoniously dumped the box onto the floor next to the ones already there. Just as he was about to retreat up the stairs, he spotted a slight glint of metal peeking through the gap between the cardboard flaps. His curiosity piqued, he leaned down and opened the box, revealing the glinting metal planchette resting on the Ouija board. Adam jumped up, startled, his heart racing as his eyes grew wide with shock. He was sure he'd thrown both the board and the planchette out months ago. How could they be here in this box?

Leaving the box behind, he dashed up the stairs, slamming the door behind him as he raced toward his dad, desperate for answers.

Below, in the corner of the basement, a dark form cloaked in darkness watched Adam's departure, its other-worldly eyes glowing with intense malevolence before vanishing. Once someone opens a door, it's hard to close it without any cracks. And a crack is all that's needed if one has enough patience.

Paint the Clown Red

Copeton Dam, northeast New South Wales, Australia

The Keelback snake slithered stealthily through the grass, its destination the murky brown discoloured body of water only a short distance away. Used to its route, it stopped in confusion when it sensed an object before it which shouldn't have been there. Lifting its head, the snake tasted the air with its flickering tongue, searching for scents in the gentle breeze. Determining the object in front was something to avoid, it changed direction and navigated around it, giving the object a wide berth. Finally, finding the water's edge, it gracefully slid into the cooling waters, making for the safety of the reeds near the centre of the dam. Unbeknownst to the snake and its colony who lived there, the object was a barrel, one of a collection, each one labeled with a warning of its toxic contents, hidden among the dense grass on the dam's edge. Their dumping had been anything but gentle, causing a rupture to form in multiple places, enabling the sludge within to escape and find its way into the once pure but muddy waters of the dam.

With anticipation bubbling inside him, Jack Roberts stood in front of the impressive display of innovative equipment and machinery. As the owner of Roberts Cosmetics, he was always looking for new opportunities to create something different and exciting to gain an edge over his competitors. The new equipment he had just gotten installed would enable him to do just that. Granted, he would have to take some shortcuts that would be frowned upon if they were ever discovered but risks sometimes had to be taken when you are aiming for the cutting edge.

Jack's reverie was interrupted by Francis, the head of clinical research, who approached nervously. Jack turned around and smiled.

"Francis, my man, are we all set to go?"

Francis slowly shook his head. The man looked worn out.

"It's not looking good, Jack; the report states the water quality is unchanged despite our best efforts."

Francis handed over the report and fidgeted nervously as Jack scanned the figures with a deepening frown. The report offered a detailed analysis of the water quality in Copeton Dam, which sat just behind the factory. Though his factory was conceivably near enough to use the waters of Lake Inverell; the cost of using Copeton Dam would be significantly lower. The problem being that they had used it as an illegal dumping ground to house the offshoots of the factory chemicals, which had since begun to leak into the dam. Since then, he had invested a significant amount of money in treating the water, hoping to make it suitable for his latest product. Francis had developed a face paint that boasted effortless application and removal, surpassing all other products on the market.

With an exasperated sigh, he lowered the papers and glared at Francis with a scowl.

"You're telling me that despite all the money I've thrown at it, the water is still unsuitable? If we have to use it the way it is, then so be it. I'm not going to waste any more money on this."

"We can't, Jack. If we use it, there's no telling what reactions people will have. Do you really want to risk the business by going ahead anyway?"

Jack's face turned beet red as anger clouded his features.

"Don't you ever tell me what to do. Your job is to research and come up with new ideas, and that's it. My business is my own, and I'll decide to take any risk I want."

Sighing, he felt his anger ebb away, and his expression shifted to one of resignation. Even as the boss, he knew he had overstepped.

"Listen, Francis, I know how much effort you've put

into this. I don't want to see it go to waste. I believe in this product; I believe in you. How about this? What if we label the face paint unsuitable for use on sensitive skin? That way, the risk will be minimized. If we start getting any reports of issues, then we can reconsider."

Despite his uncertainty, Francis nodded his head in reluctant agreement. He knew better than to argue with Jack; it was a battle he would never win.

"I'll get the ball rolling then. We should have a sample batch ready by the end of the week for trial testing and sale approval."

"Who said anything about trial testing? We're going straight to market, baby. We need to regain our market share and recoup our losses from the damn water treatment."

Francis looked at him with trepidation. Every other cosmetic he had been involved in creating had gone through clinical trials and tested on a small audience before going to a wider market.

"Jack, I don't think..."

"Okay, Francis, you do drive a hard bargain, don't you?" Jack said, his brows furrowed, and his voice filled with frustration and impatience.

"I'll give you twenty percent of the profits we make if that will keep you happy. Now, if you'll excuse me, I have some paperwork to do."

Without waiting for a response, Jack turned and hurried back upstairs toward his office, leaving Francis to stare after him in consternation.

A sigh of defeat escaped him. He would start the

manufacturing process, but he wanted no part in the fallout he knew was coming. He would hand in his resignation upon delivery of the first batch.

Paul Howard, better known as Pickles the Clown, gazed into the mirror, studying himself. These days, he could hardly recognize himself. The man staring back at him looked like a stranger and was far removed from the eager and naïve youngster he once was. Fifteen years had passed since then. The years had taken a toll on his once youthful and lively features, leaving behind a tired and weathered countenance. Years of contorting his face for his career had left him with a landscape of wrinkles and lines that told the story of his journey. The constant application of makeup and face paint he'd had to apply didn't help either.

In the early days of his career, he paid little attention to the type of face paint he used, resulting in a breakout of acne and eventually leading to scarring from a resulting infection. With all the chemicals he'd put on his face, he was surprised it hadn't done more damage than it had. So, when he'd heard of a new face paint product on the way which was supposed to revolutionize the industry, he was unconvinced, to say the least. Nevertheless, his supplier had already received some initial inventory and planned to send him a few samples in the next shipment, so he decided to give it a shot. It couldn't possibly make him look any worse after all.

Letting out a weary sigh, he grabbed the face paint and his brushes and began applying them. He had a show coming up in a few hours, the last one for the week before a few days' break. It was time to get to work.

Jack assessed the tubs of face paint, marveling at the craftsmanship. He had gone all out on the packaging for this product line. The tub had a golden color and was adorned with swirling patterns of blue. The metal itself was hardy and resistant to denting; the lettering wrapped around the tin, "Fantasy Faces," screamed premium as befitting a product that aimed to be the market leader.

Unscrewing the top of a tub labelled "Pink", he dipped his finger into the thick mixture and brought it up to the light to inspect it. Rubbing it between his fingers, he could feel the grainy mixture roll and spread easily between them. Lifting it to his face, he drew a circle on his right cheek, taking the hand mirror given to him by an anxious Francis and applying it evenly.

The mixture appeared flawless, its texture cool and velvety, devoid of any unpleasant oily or sticky sensations commonly found in other brands. He let it sit for a few minutes. Traditionally, face paint would take an hour to dry. His mixture was designed to settle in five to ten minutes, depending on the skin type it was applied to. He moved his cheek around with his hand, checking for any dryness or cracking, but it remained smooth. He lifted an unpainted finger to the face paint and traced it over the top, checking for any paint that might come off. His finger remained spotless. Francis gave him a damp cloth to clean his face, and with just a few wipes, the paint came off completely, leaving no residue. Usually, it would require soap and water to remove it and would take multiple attempts. His mixture was perfect.

He smiled broadly at Francis, handing him back the mirror and tossing him the wet rag.

"It's perfect Francis, I'll have it sent off for approval of sale. In the meantime, start contacting our wholesalers and offer them free samples. Let's get this out there as soon as possible."

He turned around, humming happily, and began his ascent back upstairs to his office.

"Sure, Jack," Francis called after him. He hesitated, his eyes fixed on the retreating figure, before mustering the courage to call out once more. "Ummm, Jack, I need to talk to you about something..."

"It'll have to wait. I'm going to head home early tonight to celebrate. I'll see you tomorrow."

Jack reached the top of the stairs and waved him off, continuing to hum to himself as he strolled toward his office. He had no intention of getting approval. He wanted his product out there, and all it was going to take was a bit of cash to do it.

Pickles stood at the exit of the "Whimsical Wonders" circus tent, shaking hands, cracking jokes and making faces, to the delight of all the children and parents as they filed out.

Pickles genuinely loved his job. There was something about bringing smiles to faces that brought a grin to his own. In a world full of stress, anxiety and money pressures, he was glad to provide solace from it all, even if it was for fifteen minutes plus sporadic appearances throughout the rest of the night.

Just as he was turning to head toward the backstage area after the last group of people had exited, there was a shy, "Hello" from outside that stopped him in his tracks.

As he turned around, a smile spread across his face upon seeing a young boy nervously smiling back at him, accompanied by his mother and father. The trio wearing worn-out and oversized clothes approached with hesitation. Offering a reassuring smile, Pickles crouched and beckoned the boy to come closer with a gentle gesture.

He could tell the trio were likely destitute, which made him all the more determined to put a smile on their faces.

"Oh, hey there," he said in an over exaggerated friendly tone, practically bursting with enthusiasm.

"Come closer, so Pickles can get a good look at you."

The young boy approached him, slow and uncertain, a shy smile flickering across his face. Behind him, his parents looked on—silent, smiling, and holding back more than words.

"What's your name, son?"

"A-Andy," the boy stuttered, unable to meet Pickles' gaze.

"Andy, now that's a nice name. Wait a minute, that's my name! Did you steal my name?"

Their eyes met, and Andy burst into laughter upon seeing the puzzled expression on Pickles' face.

"Wait just a second. I'll prove it to you. Let me just find my wallet."

With a flourish, Pickles pretended to search his uniform pockets until he revealed a seemingly endless stream of handkerchiefs, a classic clown trick.

"Oh, silly me, that's not it," Pickles said, placing his hands on his hips and staring at the handkerchief with a frown. "Let me check again."

This time, he activated a small bottle tucked away in his pocket, and a ribbon of silly string shot out, landing on Andy and catching him off guard. For a moment, Andy froze—then laughter erupted from him, wild and unfiltered, as he hopped around like a firecracker.

"Oh, oh no, oh dear, this won't do at all." Pickles stood there staring aghast at the silly string covering Andy. "Now I've really gone and done it, silly Pickles." He dropped his gaze to the ground, his lips pursed in a dramatic pout, with his shoulders drooping. Then, with a sudden spark in his eyes, he perked up. "Aha! I have an idea! How about, to make up for it, I give you.... This!"

With a smooth motion, he waved his hands and effortlessly produced tickets from a hidden pocket in his sleeve. He extended them towards Andy, his face transforming into a wide, silly grin.

Andy erupted into laughter, clapping his hands with

glee. Joy lit up his face as he dashed toward Pickles and threw his arms around him in a tight, exuberant hug.

Pickles returned the hug, his face lighting up with a genuine smile.

"I'll see you tomorrow, kiddo," he said, his voice filled with warmth as he patted him on the back with gentle affection.

Rising to his feet, he turned to the parents and handed them the tickets.

"Thank you so much," the mother said, her voice soft with gratitude. "You really didn't have to do this. Just being able to see you was enough."

"Oh, it's nothing," he said, his voice filled with warmth and reassurance.

"By the way, Andy, I'll be dedicating my performance to you. Be sure to give me a wave when I do ok?"

Andy let out a joyful squeal and bolted toward his parents, who knelt to meet him in a three-way embrace, laughter and love wrapping around them like sunlight.

Before they departed, the father looked up at Pickles and mouthed a heartfelt thank you.

Pickles watched them go, a smile lingering on his face, before he retreated to the backstage area. He really did love his job.

The next morning, Paul was jolted awake by a forceful knock on the door of his caravan. He heard Doug's booming voice calling out, "Delivery!" before his heavy footsteps receded.

Groggy and disoriented, Paul flung the bedsheets off and sat on the edge of the bed, feeling the cool floor beneath his feet. He yawned and stretched, wincing at the cracks emanating from his stiff muscles.

"Yep, definitely getting old," he grumbled to himself, feeling the stiffness in his joints before he stood up and switched on the kettle. While waiting for the water to boil, he opened the caravan door and retrieved the box left outside. Neatly printed on the side were the words "Fantasy Faces."

"Must be the new samples my supplier has been going on about," he said, tearing it open to reveal the well-presented tins of face paint within. "Looks fancy enough. Let's just see how it performs tonight."

The day passed quickly, Paul relishing the chance to relax and enjoy a rare day off. It was his usual habit to volunteer his help, even when it wasn't required of him. Doing nothing during his daytime downtime was often a struggle for him, especially after he had taken care of his props, finished his exercise routine, and rehearsed, so he was glad to do so.

Eager to experiment with the so-called revolutionary new face paint, he decided to get himself ready for the night's show a bit earlier this time. Sitting before the mirror, with the face paint tubs positioned before him, he cracked the white tub open and began liberally applying it to his cheeks and forehead. It felt surprisingly smooth and easy to apply, much easier than he was used to. He noticed it felt unusually moist, which made him a little worried. However, upon testing it, he discovered it stayed on without smudging. He was impressed. He remained so as he continued applying the face paint, taking a step back and admiring his reflection in the mirror once he finished. It looked just as good as any other night, if not better, and it had taken half the time to apply. It appeared more defined and colourful than what he was used to, which was no doubt a good thing. He made a mental note to follow up with his supplier for more of the face paint. Making the last-minute adjustments to his attire, he rose to his feet and slipped into the comically oversized clown shoes. Satisfied, he made his way to the entrance of the circus tent, ready to welcome the people pouring in for the night's show.

After ten minutes, his face became unbearably hot and prickly, causing him to fight the temptation to scratch and smudge his makeup while greeting the continuous flow of people. As the final spectator made their way past, he yielded to the irresistible urge and tenderly scratched at a bothersome patch, being cautious not to disturb the carefully applied makeup. Despite his efforts, the itch stubbornly returned the moment he lowered his hand. Beads of sweat formed on his forehead. His face felt like it was on fire, and all he wanted to do was run to his tent and wash the face paint off. He felt overwhelmed with panic. The show was about to begin, leaving him no time to wash it off and replace it. He would have to bear the discomfort and run back to his tent at the first opportunity he got once the show was over.

He wiped at the glistening sweat on his forehead, unknowingly transferring flecks of face paint into his eyes. The ringmaster had just begun his opening speech, his voice booming through the loudspeakers. He had to ready himself. Taking deep breaths to steady his nerves, he strode out at the appointed time. He blinked rapidly, trying to clear the sweat from his eyes as the bright lights illuminated his path.

Just as he was about to begin his usual routine, he suddenly found himself standing there, unable to utter a word. As the spotlight focused on him, it felt as if sharp daggers were piercing his eyes, while a wave of dizziness overwhelmed his senses. As he looked around, searching for someone to help, he spotted Andy waving at him in sheer delight, accompanied by his parents, who wore matching grins. He could feel his stomach churning as his vision blurred and distorted before his eyes. Something was moving out of the corner of his eye, but no matter which direction he looked, it remained elusive. His face felt like it was literally crawling now. He felt for his cheeks, and touched them gingerly, recoiling in terror when he felt something wriggling beneath. Desperate now, he ran his hands over his face and eyes, feeling wriggling things beneath his flesh wherever he touched. Without warning, his vision vanished in one eye, and he shuddered in horror as he sensed something wriggling loose from the tight space between his skin and his eyeball. He staggered backwards as the wriggling thing fell to the ground, his one remaining working eye searching the surface for whatever had pulled itself free. It was a worm, its creamy white, cylindrical and slender body wriggling on the ground, resembling the sinuous movements of a snake.

The sight of blood streaming from Pickles' eye-socket was met with horrified screams from the crowd, who had realized that this was not a part of the act. With unnatural swiftness, Pickles' body straightened, his posture becoming tall and rigid. His face contorted, his eyes twitching and glazing over, leaving behind a vacant expression. His arms dangled at his sides while his legs quivered uncontrollably. Every inch of exposed skin wriggled and crawled and began to swell, small pockets of blood forming beneath the surface. More and more worms fell to the ground, escaping through any orifice they could find. With a sudden anguished scream, Pickles ran with unnatural speed toward the crowd, who were now scrambling for the exit. His body was no longer his, taken over by the wriggling infestations, which continued to explore and wreak havoc within his flesh and fused with his brain.

He flung himself at the crowd, zeroing in on the nearest spectator. Raising his fist, he brought it crashing down on top of the man's head with incredible strength; the impact accompanied by a sickening crunch of compressed neck bones. As she tried to run past, he grabbed another woman by her hair, tearing it partially from her scalp and causing blood to stream down her forehead and into her eyes. In a grotesque display, he leaned forward and licked it with a worm-ridden tongue, resulting in a rain of small wriggling worms falling onto and oozing down the woman's terrified face. In a horrifying display of strength, he enclosed her head within his hands, exerting enough force to cause her skull to shatter, filling the air with a nauseating pop and a spray of pink mist, coating those unfortunate enough to be nearby in a gruesome mixture of gore and brain matter. His attacks were relentless, targeting anyone unfortunate enough to be in his vicinity as the terrified and desperate crowd attempted to flee. They resorted to tearing holes in the tent, attempting to create alternative exits to avoid the congestion, but they were no match for Pickles and the unnatural speed that he now possessed. Limbs and bodies lay scattered on the floor, a testament to his relentless onslaught, while blood stained the ground, pooling together to create a ghastly, crimson river.

With only a handful of people remaining in the circus tent, he saw a small, trembling figure near the bodies of his initial victims. Frozen in fear, Andy looked up and saw the barely human-looking form of Pickles approaching. His once goofy makeup had now transformed into a twisted, contorted visage, resembling something straight out of a nightmare. Blood and worms poured from every part of his body; a trail of the slimy, wriggling things left behind in his wake.

Without hesitation, Pickles bent down toward him, only to jerk back as a thunderous crack exploded inside the dilapidated tent. In a horrifying display, a bullet forcefully tore open his shoulder, unleashing a spray of blood and worm matter as it pierced through his infected flesh and exited on the other side.

A second blast followed, the bullet ripping through his stomach as Pickles continued to reel backward from the impact of the gunfire. In a gruesome sight, one last blast obliterated half of Pickles' head, sending bone, blood, brain matter, and worms scattering in all directions.

Pickles fell to the floor with a loud thud, his flesh splitting open upon impact, allowing squirming worms to emerge from his body.

Andy, paralyzed with shock, raised his eyes to see a pale-faced police officer drawing near. With care, the officer stooped down, scooped Andy up, and carried him outside, through the exit, into the crisp night air.

The night pulsed with the vivid hues of police and ambulances, their flashing lights casting an unsettling glow on the chaotic scene. People hurried past, their hurried footsteps and hushed whispers swallowed by the tent's opening, only to emerge moments later, visibly shaken and emptying their stomachs onto the grass.

Andy gripped the police officer's shoulder, his eyes wide as he glanced back at the tent, struggling to comprehend the events of the night and the devastating reality that he had lost his parents forever.

Parasite Research Hub, a division of the CDC,
Sydney NSW
Two days later

Lilly studied the test results, her eyes widening in growing horror. After the massacre at the Whimsical

Wonders circus in Echuca, Victoria, things had spiraled out of control. The organisms responsible, identified to be a variation of the O. Robertsi roundworm, had undergone significant mutation, resulting in rapid growth and accelerated egg production in quantities that shouldn't have been possible. They were now everywhere and spreading like wildfire, infecting people with alarming rapidity. A spread that couldn't be contained. Reports of infections were emerging from Victoria, Queensland, the Northern Territory, and as far as Perth, which was on the opposite side of the country. It shouldn't have been possible, but then again, the mutations to the roundworms were equally improbable.

Lilly, the head parasitologist at the Parasite Research Hub, a branch of the CDC, had been approached by the CDC as soon as they learned of the infections, and she had been immersed in intensive research ever since. Luckily, her advanced equipment allowed fast turn-around of results, enabling her to perform a raft of tests on what remained of the worm-riddled body of Paul "Pickles the Clown" Howard.

The latest test results in her hand had come from the cosmetic face paint. The remains of eggs, some still dormant and intact, were embedded in the paint, indicating that the origin of the organisms was the paint itself.

She picked up the phone, the weight of the conversation ahead heavy in her mind, and dialled the number for Professor Bob McCauley, the head of the CDC.

Roberts Cosmetics, Northeast New South Wales, Australia
Six months later

The warehouse stood in desolation, the foul odor of decomposing bodies permeating the air, their lifeless corpses strewn across the floor, a grim scene that would have made anyone's stomach churn had there been anyone left to witness it. Francis, the former head of the now non-existent Roberts Cosmetics, lay lifeless on a stacked crate, surrounded by a row of identical crates, each one with the label "Fantasy Faces". Throughout the country, similar warehouses lay abandoned. Cities, towns and roads lay silent, disturbed only by the crawling and slithering parasites claiming them as their own.

The CDC had been unable to stop the spread of the larvae. Their origin had been tracked down to the roundworm egg filled toxic waters of Copeton Dam, carried in by the Keelback snakes from the egg-laden vegetation surrounding it. Roberts Cosmetics had then unwittingly used the water for its new face paint, "Fantasy Faces", causing the initial outbreak. From that point forward, the roundworms, mutated by the toxic sludge that had leaked into the dam, had proven unstoppable.

For every outbreak contained, dozens more sprang up like wildfire. It wasn't long before the water supplies and food manufacturers fell victim to the worms, causing widespread panic. Once that had happened, there was no turning back. Despite Australia being in isolation, recent reports indicated that the worm infection had spread to New Zealand, Papua New Guinea, and Japan. There was a concern among scientists that the worms might have developed the ability to survive in the ocean, potentially causing infections in the sea life. As it turns out, they were right.

Echoes of the Damned

New Jersey, 30 miles from Ironwood Penitentiary.

The loud metallic jangle of the restraints filled the bus as it travelled over a particularly large pothole. Matthew grumbled to himself with irritation. At sixty-two years old, his eyesight and reflexes weren't like they used to be. He yearned for retirement. Only a few more years to go now before he could move away and buy himself and his wife Erica a quiet house somewhere near the beach to while away their twilight years. That was in the future. Right now, he had to focus on getting this rickety old bus and its cargo of human filth to their destination, the newly constructed Ironwood Penitentiary in Branchville.

This was the fifth such trip he'd made there over the past several days, slowly transferring the inmates from the soon to be closed, Clearwater Correctional Centre in Schenectady to the new facility. The journey was a two-

and-a-half-hour trip, and it was a marvel that the old bus, severely in need of a service, was still going. Thankfully, it would soon be the responsibility of the next unlucky sod who got to drive it after this one last trip so he could enjoy a much-needed few days off.

"Can you try not to hit every pothole on the road?" a voice dripping with sarcasm said from behind him through the aluminium partition.

Matthew looked in the rearview mirror and raised his middle finger at the steely-faced correctional officer, Steven.

Daniel, standing guard on the opposite side of the partition from Matthew, chuckled before Steven's glare silenced him.

With a faint smile lingering on his lips, Daniel redirected his attention to the row of prisoners, their disinterested gazes fixed on the passing landscape.

As a rookie and having only been in the job for six months, the prospect of relocating to Ironwood Penitentiary secretly excited Daniel. Despite being more remote and sparsely populated than Schenectady, he looked forward to the peace and stillness of the small community, already planning the hikes and explorations he would undertake in the nearby forests and mountains. Working with Steven was eye-opening, but even his weary and pessimistic view of his job and the residents of the penitentiary couldn't dampen his enthusiasm for his profession. Perhaps, after the ten-year gap in experience Steven had over him, his perspective would also shift, but he clung to the hope that it wouldn't.

In the second row from the back of the bus, Marcus Johnson eyed the imposing figure of Victor "Viper" Martinez seated opposite him with suspicion. Victor's constant furtive glances back and forth between Daniel and Steven spoke of trouble ahead. It was just a matter of time. Nudging the Jamaican-born Derek next to him, he leaned in and whispered, "That asshole Victor is up to something, I can smell it."

He leaned back and sniffed at the air, wrinkling his nose. "Or maybe that's just me." His eyebrows drew together, forming a deep crease of uncertainty as he leaned back in towards Derek. "It's probably me, but he's definitely up to something."

Derek glanced at him and let out a weary sigh. "You're almost due for your meds, aren't you?"

Marcus bit his lower lip, straining to think before his eyes widened as realization dawned on him. "You know what? You're right, I am! I knew there was a reason why it was starting to get so noisy in here." He raised his manacled hands, tapping his forehead.

Derek slumped in his seat, his brow furrowed with a frown as he gazed out the window. Marcus could be an okay guy when he was on his meds, but he was best avoided when they wore off. They had been promised that there would be a pill call on arrival for those who needed it, and Marcus most assuredly needed it. The sooner he was in line, waiting for his medication to be dispensed, the better it would be for everybody.

A sudden rattle of chains and the subsequent sound of them dropping to the floor captured everyone's attention as the enormous form of Victor rose, handcuff-free, from his seat and barrelled toward the startled pair of guards. Steven regained his composure enough to reach toward the taser attached to his belt, but he couldn't quite reach it in time before Victor pounced, driving his body into Steven's chest. The collision sent them crashing into the partition, causing it to emit a groan of protest.

Victor's fists came crashing down onto Steven in a relentless assault as Daniel fumbled for his baton, his heart pounding in his chest.

"Get him off me, get him off me," Steven screamed as blood spilled from his mouth, the force of Victor's blows dislodging his teeth.

With one last blow, Steven's voice was silenced. Daniel poised himself with the baton, his grip tightening as he closed the distance between him and Victor. In a split second, Victor sensed the impending danger and whirled, launching himself at Daniel, propelling both of them into the side of the bus. The collision was fierce. Daniel's body went limp upon impact, his head striking the floor and rendering him unconscious in an instant.

"Holy shit," Matthew cried, wrenching the steering wheel to the side and jamming on the brakes, hoping to send Victor off his feet to the floor. It did, but not for long. Rising to his feet, Victor pulled at the weakened partition with all his might. The deafening sound of metal grinding against metal echoed through the space, while the group of inmates behind him roared with excitement, egging him on.

With trembling hands, Matthew extended his arm towards the console, pressing the small red panic button before reaching for his two-way radio.

Victor renewed his assault on the partition and the protesting groans of the metal gave way to screeches as the metal pulled free from its rusted moorings, allowing Victor to squeeze through the opening and tear the radio handset from Matthew's grasp before he had a chance to use it.

In one swift motion, Victor's hands closed around Matthew's head, wrenching it with a sickening crunch as the neck bones gave way. Retrieving a set of keys from Steven's prone body, Victor wasted no time in unlocking the prisoners' handcuffs, the noise of the locks clicking open, drowned out by the hurried footsteps of their liberation.

When the only prisoner left to free was Jack Thompson, a convicted rapist and someone Victor had repeated run-ins with over their time in prison, Victor couldn't resist taunting him. He leered at him, dangling the set of keys in his face before snatching them away and making for the door.

"Hey, get back here, you prick!" Jack stumbled after him uselessly, his feet catching on Daniel's lifeless form as he crashed to the floor, cursing.

Victor ran out of the bus with a grin while Marcus and Derek debated their next move outside.

Victor had timed his attack on the guards to perfection. The bus had been travelling along Route 206, surrounded by the lush greenery of the Stokes State

Forest, when he had made his move. The moment Matthew hit the panic button, the escapees knew they had to move quickly, as law enforcement would be arriving soon.

With this realization in mind, Marcus and Derek quickly came to a mutual decision to stay together and make their way towards the nearby camping grounds they had noticed passing by only minutes earlier, right before Victor's ambush. Once there, their plan was to find a car and either take it through force or otherwise convince the owner to give them a lift.

Ignoring Jack's pleas for help as he stumbled out of the bus, the pair turned and headed into the forest at a brisk jog. They could see Victor ahead of them crashing his way through the trees, uncaring of the obvious traces of his passing he was leaving behind.

"Do you think he's headed toward the same campground we are?" Derek said between gasps for air.

"Hmmmm... maybe. Hey, let's ask him!"

Before Derek could protest, Marcus yelled out in an overly loud voice. "Hey Victor, are you headed for the campsite?"

Derek smacked his forehead in frustration and let out a deep sigh. Perhaps it wasn't such a good idea to escape with Marcus.

Victor came to an abrupt halt and spun around to face them, irritation etched on his face. Right as he was about to answer, his head snapped to the left, cocking it to the side as if he detected a faint sound that demanded his attention.

"Do you hear something?" Marcus yelled out, oblivious to how loud he was being.

Victor remained quiet, a puzzled look on his face, before his features shifted to one of comprehension, nodding as if acknowledging a secret conversation only he could hear. Paying no attention to the duo, he sprinted deeper into the forest, headed in a direction opposite to the campsite.

"Was it something I said?" Marcus said, his face crumpled with hurt.

"Come on," Derek mumbled, giving Marcus a small shove.

The pair pressed on, navigating their way up a steep incline, the thick fern undergrowth making each step a challenge. Sweat poured down their bodies as they struggled in the cloying summer humidity of the forest, swatting at annoying insects as they worked their way through the vegetation. Finally, after what felt like an eternity, they emerged from the sea of ferns into a section of the forest with majestic oak trees, their branches reaching toward the sky. A delicate layer of leaves carpeted the ground beneath their feet, each one curling and veined.

Derek, exhausted, collapsed against one of the nearby oaks, sliding down to the ground and gasping for breath as he tried to regain his strength. Marcus, still buzzing with energy, settled down happily beside him, his eyes darting with interest around the forest.

"How long do you think until we get to the campsite?"

"Too long," Derek grumbled, closing his eyes as he continued to draw in breaths.

"Do you think anyone else is headed that way?"

"I don't..." Derek's words were drowned out by a short-lived scream, its abrupt end leaving behind a haunting silence.

Victor crashed through the trees, uncaring of the noise he was making, his focus completely on reaching the location the voices were insisting he reach. From the instant he heard them, he was immediately captivated. Their soothing tone had a calming effect on his soul, as if a weight had been lifted off his shoulders. They spoke just a few words, but their strength, kindness, and reassurance made him feel safe and comforted. He yearned to follow their directions, feeling an intense desire for nothing else. They promised him salvation, a lifeline to cling to in his darkest moments. Freedom from the torment of dreams, flashbacks, and self-mutilation that had haunted him for so long. What he had to do in his life, what he had got caught up in as muscle for the mafia, couldn't be escaped no matter how much he ran. Promising relief from it all, the voices enveloped his mind with a comforting aura of security and safety. In exchange for that relief and the promise of more, he was willing to do whatever they asked of him.

Eventually crashing through into a space bare of trees, Victor came to a halt and surveyed his surroundings. He was in a natural clearing, but it was what lay in the center that caught his attention. Surrounded by withered, yellowing vegetation, an expansive, darkened circle rested, its desolation punctuated by the absence of life, leaving only dirt and rock behind. In the very center, a gaping hole loomed, its darkness inviting and mysterious. It looked to be roughly two meters in diameter from where Victor was standing. It was from this location that the voices in Victor's head originated, urging him to walk toward them. With each obedient step, the voices grew clearer and more forceful, overpowering his mind's warning signals that something was amiss.

Had Victor been able to tune out the voice's instructions for a moment, he would have heard what wasn't there: a silence so complete it felt curated, as if nature itself had recoiled. There was no sound of wings flapping, birds chirping, or creatures scurrying through the bushes —only the gentle brush of the wind against the tree leaves. Instead, his attention was fixed solely on the large circular hole that loomed closer and closer as he approached until he reached its edge, everything else fading into insignificance. As if on cue, the sun appeared from behind the clouds, sending its rays cascading into the abyss before him. Victor sank to his knees, transfixed by what he was seeing.

A spiralling pile of bones lay beneath the hole, with the top of the pile appearing to be about sixty to seventy feet away. The foundation appeared to be made of animal bones in different stages of decomposition, suggesting they had been there for a significant amount of time. Most of the heap was made up of bones from birds, marsupials, deer, and bears. But as he looked closer, he noticed the distinct shape of human skulls near the top, their gleaming white appearance indicating they were a more recent addition.

A gentle blue light started pulsing beneath the pile of bones, casting menacing reflections on the cave walls, and Victor couldn't help but take a deep breath, his eyes filled with excitement. This was what he was here for. With each breath, he felt the weight of his old life slipping away, making room for the possibilities of his new beginning.

"Viccccctoooooooooooorrrrr", in unison, a chorus of voices called out, their melodic tones enveloping Victor in a comforting embrace and filling him with a soothing warmth. Their collective voice embodied love, acceptance, and a sense of belonging, and he wholeheartedly embraced it, allowing the accompanying presence to enter his mind.

Filled with a clear sense of duty and purpose, he rose to his feet. His master was hungry, and that just wouldn't do. At the sound of rustling leaves, his head snapped towards the tree line where Samuel Carter, one of his fellow escapees, anxiously stared back at him.

"Hey man, do you know where we are? How do we get out of here? This place just doesn't seem to end."

Victor froze and stared at him, as if unsure of how to react, before his lips curved into a gentle, inviting smile that radiated warmth. "It's your lucky day. I just found a way out. It's just over here, beyond that tree line." He indicated the direction behind him.

"Thank fuck, I was beginning to think I'd never get out of here," Samuel said with relief as he emerged from the trees and approached Victor.

"Anyone else with you?" Victor asked, his tone strangely hopeful.

"Nah, man, I'm a loner. I saw a couple of guys a few minutes ago run up there." He gestured toward the hill in the distance. "They were saying something about finding a higher vantage point to scout the area."

Victor nodded at him, with a slight smile on his lips.

"Hey, what's that?" Samuel's eyes widened with curiosity as he approached the dark hole in the centre of the clearing.

"Oh yeah, that. It looks like something used it as a dumping ground for bones," Victor said, stepping aside to let Samuel move ahead, watching him as he crouched down at the edge of the hole.

"Jesus, what the hell did that?"

"Let me show you," Victor said, casually shoving him off the edge and sending him plummeting down the hole.

Samuel's scream tore through the air, ending abruptly as his body slammed headfirst into the bone pile below. The cave answered with a brittle chorus of snapping—old fractures reawakened, fresh ones born. Above, Victor watched, his grin gleaming with quiet satisfaction.

With a sharp scream, Samuel's descent came to a sudden halt as he slammed headfirst onto the top of the bone pile. The cave echoed with a chorus of bones snapping, both old and new. Above, Victor watched, his grin gleaming with quiet satisfaction.

The blue glow returned, pulsing with renewed vigour. With a nauseating sucking sound, Samuel's flesh was stripped from his bones, sloughing off and seeping into the gaps in the bone pile, drawn downwards to the thing hiding beneath. A few minutes later, all that remained of Samuel was an empty skeleton encompassed in the remains of his tattered prison uniform.

The radiant blue light gradually faded as a surge of gratefulness washed over Victor's thoughts, leaving him in a state of serene tranquillity. An addictive sensation for a desperate mind in need of respite. The feeling brought about a call for more people to join Samuel in the depths and a guarantee of greater salvation.

"Moooooooooorrrrrrrrrreeeeeee," the voices chorused, with Samuel's voice now part of the blend.

Victor nodded in silence and turned toward the hills, where Samuel had mentioned two of the escapees had gone.

"What the hell was that?" Startled, Derek leaped to his feet, his eyes widening as he turned towards the source of the piercing scream.

"I think you mean, who the hell was that?" Marcus corrected, rising to his feet to join him.

Ignoring him, Derek darted off through the trees, the

rustling of leaves accompanying his determined sprint towards the now dormant sound.

"Was it something I said?" Marcus murmured, puzzled, his eyebrows raised quizzically.

By the time he started following, he could barely hear Derek's hurried movements through the forest in the distance. His pursuit was short-lived when the sudden sound of heavy footsteps stomping through the trees and cursing rapidly approached him and he halted, unsure of what to do.

The panting figure broke through the thicket before him, and Marcus froze, recognizing the thin, wiry form of Daniel, the corrections officer.

"Oh shit," Marcus exclaimed, his face softening into a nervous smile as he lifted his hands, palms out in surrender.

Daniel froze, his eyes widening in surprise before he scrambled for his taser and baton, unsure of which one to use.

"Stay right there," he rasped, breath hitching. Blood streaked his pallid face, bruises blooming where it had struck the bus floor. He moved as if every joint protested.

Seeing Marcus frozen in place, he took a chance—bracing one arm against the rough trunk of a nearby elm while his other hand, trembling, kept the taser trained on him.

"Looks like you need a doc there, sir," Marcus pointed out.

Daniel was about to reply when screams once again filled the forest, diverting both of their attention.

"People sure love to scream around here," Marcus remarked in annoyance. "Don't they know that screams draw attention? Not a great idea when you're trying to escape." His head shook with visible disdain, his brows furrowing and his lips curling into a scowl.

Daniel's brows knit together in brief confusion, but he drew one final deep breath, steadying himself. "Get in front of me. Do not run. Do not deviate. And do not make any sudden movements. You got me?"

"Yes, sir," Marcus said with a gulp, his eyes lowered in a display of compliance.

"Now move," Daniel said, giving Marcus a firm push with his baton towards the direction of the frantic screams.

"Ummm, excuse me, sir, aren't we supposed to be going away from the screams, not towards them?"

"Just shut your mouth and move," Daniel said, jabbing him once more with the baton.

Their swift pace through the forest created a symphony of crunching twigs and swirling leaves beneath their feet. The sun's waning power signaled the onset of evening, casting long shadows and making it more difficult to navigate the uneven terrain filled with roots and branches. The forest in this area was ancient, with towering trees and a dense canopy that only allowed a few rays of fading sunlight to filter through. Moments earlier, the screams had come to an end, and as they walked into a clearing, the sun's last rays illuminated a harrowing scene, almost as if drawing attention to its horror.

Victor was dragging Steven's body by his hands toward a large hole in the ground, next to which lay the bodies of another couple of inmates. Blood soaked the ground where Victor had dragged Steven and the inmate's bodies out of the woods, leaving no question that they were dead.

With a sudden cry, the bushes parted to the left of Marcus and Daniel as Derek burst through, heading straight toward Victor. With a final tug, Victor hauled Steven beside one of the inmates, then turned to face the oncoming Derek—his smile cold and deliberate.

Derek had almost made it to him when Victor reached behind his back and produced a taser. With a casual raise of his arm, he aimed at Derek's chest and pulled the trigger. The device crackled to life with a sharp electric buzz. Twin prongs shot out, their thin wires trailing behind, and struck Derek in the chest with a dull thud. The electrical current shot through into Derek's body, and he convulsed helplessly, his muscles locked in a rigid, uncontrollable spasm. The air was heavy with the scent of ozone as Derek collapsed to the ground, struggling to breathe.

"Derek!" Marcus shouted, worry sharp in his voice as he broke into a run toward his friend.

"Marcus, wait!" Daniel called out, eyes wide with shock as he struggled to make sense of what he was seeing.

With a wicked smile playing on his lips, Victor directed his gaze towards Marcus, who was drawing near. Their eyes met as Victor nonchalantly lifted his boot and brought it crashing down on Derek's neck, the sickening sound of crunching bones causing Marcus's heart to sink. Derek gurgled weakly, trying to draw in breath through his ruined neck before stilling. Marcus, seething with rage, balled his fists and, with a rush of adrenaline, launched himself at Victor's legs, hoping to knock the larger man off balance. Instead, it only jarred him, the impact causing a slight stumble before he regained his balance and stepped down onto Marcus's outstretched hand. Try as he might to free himself, his fingers remained trapped beneath Victor's foot. Victor pressed harder, the pain surging past unbearable—until his fingers gave way with a sickening snap. Marcus screamed as agony tore through his arms in a violent burst.

Victor looked down at him, his forehead glistening with a thin layer of perspiration, his facial muscles twitching involuntarily. His foot loosened as spasms seized his body, causing him to retreat and clutch his face with quivering hands, as if tormented.

Seizing the opportunity, Marcus lunged forward, tackling Victor once more, this time succeeding and sending them both sprawling to the ground with a heavy thud.

Marcus's face contorted with fury, hate, and anger, as it turned a deep shade of crimson. The dwindling potency of his medication left him defenseless against the relentless voices in his head, causing his mind to descend into chaos, losing control. With a guttural roar, he drove his fists with as much force as he could muster into Victor's head, each punch landing with brutal precision.

Victor's face became a grotesque mask of blood and bruises as Marcus's fist continued to rain down on him, the sound of bone crunching under his fists filling him with satisfaction and driving him on. Victor's head lolled to the side, but he didn't stop. The sound of wet, meaty thuds of flesh meeting bone filled the silent clearing, surreal in its intensity.

With one last blow, Marcus sat back to catch his breath and surveyed his handiwork. Victor's face was a pulpy mess, his head no longer symmetrical, shards of bone and brain fluid leaking onto the ground beneath.

"What... what have you done?" Daniel said in a trembling voice behind him.

Marcus rose to his feet and faced him calmly. "Exactly what needed to be done." His face, once filled with rage, now appeared devoid of any emotion. "The voices they..." He stopped speaking mid-sentence, his brows furrowed with confusion.

Something was speaking to him, but it wasn't the same familiar voices he had just heard. This was something foreign, an invasive presence that was trying to weave its way into his mind. It was pleading with him, the desperate tone of one voice standing out amidst the chorus.

"Samuel?" he muttered out loud, his face twitching as a cacophony of strange voices and his own fought for control of his mind.

"Samuel? What the fuck are you talking about?" Daniel's voice quivered with nervousness as he stepped back, his finger gripping the trigger of the charged taser.

"Samuel, he... He's talking to me," Marcus whispered, as he stumbled backwards, his hands gripping his head, a low, guttural groan escaping his throat.

He felt a sudden recoil as the presence in his head retreated, frustrated by his resistance.

Rocking back and forth, drained by the intrusion and subsequent withdraw, Marcus slowly lifted his head in time to see Daniel pushing the prone form of Steven and the inmate who he now recognised as Carlos Ramirez down into the hole. The chilling sound of snapping bones reverberated from the hole as their bodies crashed onto the bone pile.

"What... what are you doing?"

"It needs to feed," Daniel said in a monotone voice, moving towards Victor's body, pulling it by its legs and draping them over the hole before giving it a heave to join the others.

"Wh... What...?"

An intense blue glow emanating from the hole interrupted him. Approaching with utmost caution, he joined Daniel at the edge and beheld the gruesome spectacle unfolding before his eyes. The flesh of the bodies was mercilessly tearing away from their bones, causing a torrent of blood to cascade down the heap and seep through the cracks, heading towards the mysterious glowing entity underneath.

Marcus's face turned pale as he glanced at Daniel, who remained fixated on the hole with an eerie, unnaturally twitchy smile.

"What the hell is doing that? What's down there?"

Daniel turned to him, his jaw contorting in erratic, unnatural movements, as the entity below fought to maintain its grip on him while feeding simultaneously.

"Something ancient, something from the stars and beyond. It needs us, you see. It needs us so it can grow, so it can take life and give it to its own kind who are more worthy."

Stepping backwards, Marcus's lips trembled, as if struggling to form words, cold shivers of fear shooting down his spine.

"I'm going crazy. I have to be. I need my medication, that's what it is. Yes, that's it, this isn't real, this isn't real."

"Yes, it is," Daniel said, moving toward him with sudden unnatural speed. Like a marionette under the control of an unseen puppeteer, his movements were rigid and devoid of any natural fluidity. He snatched Marcus by the collar with ease, hoisting him into the air before tossing him towards the illuminated edge of the hole.

"No, wait..." Marcus cried out, frantically scanning his surroundings for any object he could use as a makeshift weapon. Lying a few feet away from him was the abandoned taser Daniel had dropped when whatever it was had taken control of him. With a desperate scramble, he reached out toward it, his fingertips grazing its surface, only to have all feeling ripped away by a brutal impact on his back. Standing over him, Daniel raised his baton above his head and swept it down with a whoosh, this time onto the back of Marcus's head, sending blood and bone flying. With one last protesting groan, Marcus passed into oblivion as Daniel continued his relentless assault, blood splattering with every blow, painting a morbid canvas on the ground. Bones continued to shatter as Daniel kept up his attack, the baton a weapon of death dripping with the crimson evidence of its lethal efficiency.

With a twisted smile, Daniel finally tossed the baton aside and admired his handiwork. His face had taken on a pallid, almost translucent quality, veins visible beneath the surface like dark, twisted roots.

He hauled Daniel's lifeless body to the edge of the hole, then unceremoniously shoved him down onto the growing pile of his master's victims. Once more, the blue glow intensified with pleasure as it hungrily drained its fresh victim of flesh and blood.

Daniel turned to face the woods, moving forward with a robotic, mechanical precision.

For a brief moment, something stirred behind Daniel's vacant eyes. A memory, fragments of a scene. The crackle of a campfire, with his friends surrounding it. His sister's laughter. Marshmallows burning on sticks. His steps faltered as a breeze whispered through the leaves of the trees surrounding him, as if trying to remind him of who he was. But as soon as it had appeared, the warmth of the memory faded, swallowed by the cold, alien need of the thing below. He resumed walking, steady and unrelenting. The hunt had only just begun. His master was still hungry.

Deep below, in the safety of its home surrounded by the bones of its victims, the entity stirred, its body renewed from the nutrients it had absorbed.

Its large bulbous form lifted itself from the ground, hovering a few inches above it. The thing's circular body had tough, leathery green skin, its delicate tendrils, reminiscent of octopus limbs, extended toward the ground, each one, covered in a thick layer of delicate sensory nubs, as they searched the ground beneath it, sensing the surface it couldn't see. Beneath heavyset bony ridges, a thick gold film covered its large, unblinking eyes. Round holes beneath took the place of where its nostrils should have been. A large open maw ringed with sharp teeth served as its mouth. It had a body covered in bony spikes, creating a menacing appearance. With no need for legs, it relied on its innate ability to levitate, staying just a few inches above the surface.

Traveling down the small tunnel system it and its kind had constructed, the entity's waving tentacles served as its sensory organs, detecting the texture of the surrounding surface. Reaching its destination, it spilled out into a large, cavernous chamber. Enormous, semi-transparent egg sacs adorned the walls, their thick, veiny skin pulsating and trembling with the movement of the life inside. With measured fluidity, the entity made its way toward a cluster of smaller eggs. Its tentacles caressed the surface of the nearest one, emitting a mesmerizing blue glow as it passed on the precious vitamins and nutrients it had absorbed, fueling the growth of new life. The chamber was a bustling hub as similar organisms entered and exited through a network of intricate tunnels, each leading to a bone pile similar to its own.

The sound of mewling, otherworldly cries filled the cavern from newly hatched spawn. Their numbers were growing. Soon, they would rise to claim the surface as their own.

ABOUT THE AUTHOR

A horror fan since childhood, Ian embraces his inner geek with pride, his dedication displayed in the intimidating collection of horror novels and video games that threaten to take over his living space.

He is mad for all things Alien, Star Wars, and cats, his furry companions always there to keep him company as he scribbles down his latest ideas.

He's a father in Melbourne, Australia, sharing his home with his partner, two stepdaughters, and four cats. The sheer number of furry and human companions in his life might be enough to drive anyone a little crazy.

You can follow his writing journey on Facebook at Ian Gielen - Author

Also by Ian Gielen

Horror Novella:

Saving Tommy

Unholy Blood

Anthologies:

Devour the Rich (Published by Above the Rain Collective)

Cryptid Codex (Published by Crimson Cult Media)

Warning: Wicked Web (Published by Crimson Cult Media)

Invasion of the Saucer-Men from Mars! (Published by Specul8 Publishing)

Attack of the Colossal Creatures from Planet X (Published by Specul8 Publishing)

Books of Horror Community Anthology Vol 4 Part 1 (Published by Books of Horror)

Petting Boo! (Published by Wicked Shadow Press)

Christmas of the Dead: Krampus Kountry (Published by Wicked Shadow Press)

Apocalyptales: Judgement Day (Published by Wicked Shadow Press)

Flash of the UnDead (Published by Wicked Shadow Press)

Flash of the Dead: Requiem (Published by Wicked Shadow Press)

Femme Fatale Flashes (Published by Wicked Shadow Press)

Masks of Sanity: The Monster Within (Published by Wicked Shadow Press)

Children of the Dead: Lost Lullabies (Published by Wicked Shadow Press)

Halloweenthology: Trick-Or-Treat (Published by Wicked Shadow Press)

Flash of the Dead: Halloween '24 (Published by Wicked Shadow Press)

Halloweenthology: Friar's Lantern (Published by Wicked Shadow Press)

Blink of an Eye (Published by CultureCult Magazine & Press)

Merry Creepsmas: The Green Book (Published by Wicked Shadow Press)

Cooks of Horror

Sleeve of Hearts

Coming Soon:

Mother of Mine (Novel)